Praise for Meredith Quartermain's *Vancouver Walking*,
winner of the 2006 BC Book Prize for Poetry

The Globe and Mail [Margaret Christakos]
"Packing a centuries-wise arsenal of research, Quartermain's poetic
tour ... reads the downtown's every street sign and historical plaque
to invoke not vagaries of weather or a sensitive narrator's emotional
landscape, but the lived epic of how specific native soil became ap-
propriated to a condition of contemporary real estate."

Monday Magazine [Marc Christensen]
"With *Vancouver Walking,* Meredith Quartermain enters the esteemed
literary company of George Bowering, Daphne Marlatt, Frank Davey,
Jeff Derksen and others who have written the multitudinous city,
exploring Vancouver as a moving target for poetry.... Under Quar-
termain's gaze, even the most local Vancouver story becomes a link
to the greater world, transforming the city into a cosmopolis made
of the mad whirls of history, in constant motion with the fates of its
living (and long dead) millions."

Arc Poetry Magazine [Chris Jennings]
"These are prominently public poems, urban poems, and Quarter-
main gears her poetic to serve and to explore her particular public
space.... The reward is an appreciation of local history's more than
local consequence and a vision of living in history as an inevitable
consequence of living in cities."

Vancouver Review [Trevor Boddy]
"Quartermain is an obsessive observer and re-describer of Vancouver
.... [C]oncise in her language ..., Quartermain follows in the foot-
steps of Lisa Robertson's brilliant poetic perambulations of Vancou-
ver urban landscapes."

Seattle Stranger [Charles Mudede]
"In *Vancouver Walking* information crowds the street, historical facts and
economic data rush toward you. The beauty of the poems in Quar-
termain's book is the beauty of information."

PoetryReviews.ca [Jenna Butler]
"Her meticulously subtle descriptions of the ignorance, racism, and
injustice that characterize so much of the history of the west coast of
Canada draw the reader in.... Aside from this carefully-developed
layering of place, the *Vancouver Walking* series quietly reveals human-
ity giving way beneath a new age of industry."

Nightmarker

Meredith Quartermain

NeWest Press

N

W

For Jenna

Meredith Quartermain

E

Nightmarker | S | Meredith Quartermain

Library and Archives Canada Cataloguing in Publication

Quartermain, Meredith, 1950–
Nightmarker / Meredith Quartermain.
Poems.
ISBN 978-1-897126-34-9
I. Title.
PS8583.U335N53 2008   C811'.6   C2008-902310-2

Editor for the Board: Douglas Barbour
Cover and interior design: Natalie Olsen
Author photo: Andrea Auge

NeWest Press acknowledges the support of the Canada Council for the Arts, the Alberta Foundation for the Arts, and the Edmonton Arts Council for our publishing program. We also acknowledge the financial support of the Government of Canada through the Book Publishing Industry Development Program (BPIDP).

NeWest Press
201.8540.109 Street
Edmonton, Alberta T6G IE6
780.432.9427
newestpress.com

No bison were harmed in the making of this book.
We are committed to protecting the environment and to the responsible use of natural resources. This book is printed on 100% recycled, ancient forest-friendly paper.

1 2 3 4 5 11 10 09 08
printed and bound in Canada

Meredith
Quartermain
2008

NeWest Press

A thing done is not simply done but is re-done or pre-done. It is at once commemorative, magical, and prospective.

Charles Olson,
The Special View of History

Sir,

I begin my search for passage, my moby dream. Points, *situs* in a written city, where the speaker is a public square for festivals and processions dancing, disintegrating, marching *palabras, parole, mots*. A Piazza Navona for markets, chariot races, and the fountains of popes who taxed bread, and burned philosophers. To speak is to navigate a vast submarine forum for *agones*: researches, minds, wills, uprisings, reigns of terror mired in crazy inferno. To speak is to echolocate — dreaming, unconscious city, written pathways shaping the letters to follow. From the chuman, comes the chimp and the human. From the amniote come the sauropsid dinosaurs and birds, the synapsid dogs, elephants, and armadillos. There's no going back, only forward in the writing / walking castle with knees, elbows, chimneys, colonnades, balconies, stairs, dumbwaiters, trundling beeping along, a great cyborg camel, so convoluted the Human can never catalogue all the moving parts let alone figure their levers and linkages. To speak is to set out like a knight to good deeds, where the goods trade on every exchange.

Sir, I go turtle, language-house on back, two shells — words and senses — bound in turtle flesh, a sign in mindless systems. I sleep-walk dreaming a moby dream of awake. Something human beyond the anthill. Where everything is UN-realized, opened to its illusory value — every pediment and frieze, every chapel and apse, every tuxedo and pajama, every *whereas* and *I do* hung on the racks of Value Village.

Seeking north by northeast,
Geo, Vancouver

DISCOVERY AT SEA | I |

Conception occurs in bothies and hutments, cabins and bungalows. A corpus of hatchling citizens, poll clerks, returning officers. Hear hear — an election. Will it be Maclean, the land agent, or Alexander, the mill-manager, for mayor? For tomorrow's metropolis, unlimited. In the courtroom with its doors to jail-cells, Major Johnson administers the oath to the realtor. *Et voilà* un mayor. His Worship swears in aldermen, the first council of embryonic city — its Roman grid already sucking placental earth. Treasurer, Solicitor, Police Magistrate emerge from chrysalids. Mr. Hemphill of Hemphill Auto Schools for Poundkeeper. City Clerk opens notebook. Minuting automatic transmission.

First council hies across to Sunnyside saloon, among brass and glass, among watch-chains and waistcoats, buttoned flies, bowlers, porkpies and Homburgs, far from the ladies' parlour. Here in the blue haze of tobacco, the thump of mugs on wood and boots on rail, howdy handshakes and steely taciturn eyes, embryonic city dreams its double helix of proto by-laws, proto assessment rolls. No money in the coffers?! Round up some drunk and disorderly malefactors. Your Worship, take the bench, try the cases! The reputation of this young and beautiful maiden's at stake! Her honour, the coffers!

Proto city hall: the police station. After the great fire a tent at Alexander Street and Carrall (he bargained three hundred sixty thousand square miles of forest and aboriginals into Canada, in exchange for the Road). From tent to Oppenheimer Bros., wholesale grocers, then Market City Hall on the edge of forest: a little medieval castle. Roman arches and twin turrets wearing flat-sided French conical hats — guild town escaped from feudal serfdoms. Out of the pan into the spider-web. Infant city moves in with Molson's Bank, the Holden Building, a ten-storey skyscraper — Corinthian columns clapped on its forehead — and dreams of growth, dreams a tranceful infant sleep, zoned for science, art and business. Silent mouths of 50th floors catching airplanes on their tongues. Clean-cut concrete cliffs rising to heaven, to refine and sculpt *homo harmonious.*

Museum I Here is the museum among its grounds. Fields of clipped grass, where rainforest and beach rushes used to be, facts and data still permitting an old stream its rocky way to the sea, past small platforms and hedged shrubs — the mind weighs in reaching for a decision, an action, a purpose.

Here is the walk-in diorama. Its brewery silos and Seaforth Armories. Its bridge named for old naval officer Burrard, that humps its back over a False Creek — its giant concrete feet planted firmly in the village of Snauq where from time immemorial Squamish came to fish. *From there I saw Vancouver burn,* the last chief told the Archivist. They searched among ruins for nails. That would fasten anything to its grounds.

Flotillas of ducks and geese covered the sheltered lagoon, which was not false, rising into the sky in clouds, and people corralled fish with fences of vine-maple driven into the mud. *Whiteman's food change everything,* the Archivist wrote the Chief's words. *Everywhere whiteman goes he change food, China, other place, he always change food where he goes.* Crossing the grounds with Ogden, McNicoll and Whyte, the CPR VPs, and their lawyer Creelman, when the Company ran its track through.

The last Squamish left Snauq the morning of April 11, 1913. Ancestors dug up, moved up coast near the Squamish River. The graveyard covered with silos of beer and the armories' medieval battlements. *The orchard went to ruin, the fences fell down, the houses were destroyed,* the Archivist recorded. As though signalling a land destined for breweries, *a few hops survived till the building of Burrard Bridge.* Every spring in old Snauq, the Shakespeare powwow throws up its teepees.

Here is the museum. Among the grounds. A solitary totem pole, a hundred feet high. *Dedicated* with cast brass plaque *in a ceremony … October 15, 1958 … a memorial to British Columbia's centennial year … an exact replica of one carved for Queen Elizabeth II by Chief Mungo Martin of the Kwakiutl Nation* — 10 Kwakiutl tribes figured on the pole.

I like that one, the Queen Elizabeth (a.k.a. Lieutenant Governor) said, flipping through the Hudson's Bay Catalogue. Let's have that one, for the centennial. Yes, your Majesty, I'll arrange for a copy to be carved. And they raised a Kwakiutl pole in Squamish country to stand for England taking the land.

Sir,

I write of organized crime. Humans draw lines in the sand, which THEY will not cross. *Terrorists attacked the World Trade Center and we will defeat them by expanding and encouraging trade.* "We" will give them beads and trinkets for a cloak of sea otters, looking-glasses for a mantle of cedars, calico for a run of sockeye. "We" will give them bouncing breasts, Harley bikes and hot tubs for celestial spheres. Safe injection sites, cigarettes, taco chips, sitcoms, dirt bikes, midriffs for all we've made impossible.

In this twilight of the Dark Ages, chronometers are failing, and planets have wandered. Organic / inorganic axes are ceasing, as Humans run like ants among hills of sugar. Where and how is the fugitive when bravery is cowardice and freedom slavery. I navigate trade winds with eclipses and lunar distances parallel sailing for a moby dream.

Yet, suppose I find a filament of sense or an ocean of thrashings, how will I make it out to you? in these leaking jollyboats and whalers rowed by one-oared drunken boatswains who circle crazily, bailing themselves out, and at last spill the cargo into the mud a few steps from the launch point. Picking up splices in winding alleys, I fend off thieves, and arrive at your doorstep, clothes torn, face bleeding, long after you've shipped out.

Hoping this finds you,
Geo, Vancouver ·

DISCOVERY AT SEA | 2 |

Magnetic North | City blocks are islands weathered by streets. Footsteps. Time. How navigate? A $5 compass or $10 one, Army & Navy. You get the directions you pay for. Clerk's got a long-stemmed rose on her arm. *This side please, come round this side* — loudly to hunched elderlies. Wouldja put this in a bag please. *No, you have to buy it first.* (It's $3 of potting soil.) A man holds some pill bottles. Depending on where you are, magnetic north wanders from true north. Army & Navy clerk studies the pills. $44.57. Why's it so much? *Each of these is $10. You got 3, that's $30, plus Aqua Velva, and you got tax.* Large objects like buildings make the compass deviate. Outside Army & Navy past the yellow-jacketed security guard: Couldja spare 50¢ for a coffee. She says it over and over. Ripped tights, face the colour of bruises. Here's a toonie. The $10 compass says West Hastings's going northish. Knives, wristwatches, lighters, steel-rimmed glasses, belt buckles — they all cause deviation. In the window of Save-on-Meats, pork necks are 79¢. Chicken backs 39¢. Beef hooves $1.89.

Veer off, 30 degrees northeast suffering possible deviation from a lamp post. Maybe deviants, delinquents, eccentrics qualify for standard deviation, the square root of the average square of all deviancy. From the norm, the correctly proper, the fitting, the aptly pertinent, the importantly focal, the key, the secret, the recipe. At the steam clock with its five little steaming chimneys, chains of hooks and steel balls slowly travel up, then drop to gear its pendulum and frantic spinning wheels. A sandwich board points to a telephone booth saying Language Repair Shop. Yes, we fix tergiversators.

Sir,

The very circumscribed view that I have of the country renders it impossible to form the most distant idea of the situation in which I have become stationary, whether made of islands or arms of the sea. In value village, the fitting rooms say Men or Women, Sir or Madam, He or She. Us and Them. None are marked Shades or Geoids. And the country is thus infinitely divided. Yet I persist.

My researches from Cultural Inlet drive along the western channel I call Perception, where tides are favorable to conjectures. This channel branching off in two directions, one stretching northward, one southward, containing many intricate sunken rocks and rocky islets, a network of little eyes widening its speculations through agitated tides along the eastern shore.

Sir, I am becalmed by automobiles. Humans run bolt-wrenches rapid fire and punch barrels of oil. How do they know they are Human? and not animal as Raccoon? Operating the Main Frame with surgical strikes, then unscrewing their masks for transplants.

Your steadfast and humming servitude,
Geo, Vancouver

DISCOVERY AT SEA | 3 |

The Raws

The Raws I If city is figure what is ground? 20,000 tons of brown sugar, four storeys high, land gifted from city to sugar factory — with tax breaks and free water. Every few minutes, a man with an earth mover scoops three tons of raws into a hopper.

1890s: men hauled 700-pound baskets from ships. Picked and sawed like miners at brown boulders in cavernous warehouses. Factory paid managing director $5000 a year, plus $20,000 bonus in 1892, same year it paid $18,000 in dividends.

Cutting up, distributing pieces, classifying, parting, disuniting, subjecting to division.

Can you divide figure from ground? What's individual and not divisible?

1916 $400,000 in dividends. 1917 280% dividend. Same year factory workers struck three months for a 10% raise.

Bonusing: (1) rewards to directors or managers; (2) the use of public money to set up private companies. 1890-city raising $30,000 with 5% debentures, buying sugar-land from mayor's land company, hiring contractors to clear it. On plantations, thirty slaves with hoes trenched two acres a day, planting cane — 1.4 million Cormantins, Papaws, Ibos, Bantus shipped to sugar islands — 300,000 dying at sea.

Outside sugar shed, *Ocean Harmony* nestles in dock, seawater playing reflections on her steel hull. Men in white lab-coats, men in overalls, men in hardhats move in and out company buildings doing their refining.

After laws against slavery, plantations took indentured coolies from India. Fijians didn't want sugar-cane jobs, British-refined wife recalls in company history. Sugar factory bought 387 men, 152 women and 90 children all "contracted" to Fiji plant. The company supplied milk to children *living in the lines.*

Port City ❙ *Yo! Where you going* (security guard, Clark trucking overpass — chair parked mid street, tractors roaring round the clover-leaf in the blaring sun). Public Viewing Area. *Okay, just around the corner.*

Just around the corner the public can be seen. But public viewing permanently closed for demolition. No public, except half-hour slide-show Wednesdays.

Sit in the parking lot of the former public with the whoosh of the grain silo's blue and green ducts. Green shipping containers saying Capital. All port access restricted to haulers. K-Line. Hapag-Lloyd, Tex, Hanjin, China Shipping. Lined up at seven gates. Forklift snubs up to container stack, grapples box-car Cosco 40 feet up. Swivels. Puffs diesel as it sets load on trailer. Truck pulls out. Triton, says the box. Every 3 minutes, trucks roll off with box-cars of sweat-shop jackets, dinnerware, computers, teddy-bears, shoes, living-room sets.

Boxes in human heads same corrugated steel. Orange frames, zig zag catwalks above warehouses. Hoisting human-head containers, forklifted to long-haul tractors, shipped to other human heads. Is this the human infestation — to ants — to universe? Is there no escape? No outside to this?

Humans vs ants. If ants controlled the world and not humans — could humans do something different than leaf-cutters building highways, hauling leaves, tunnelling streets, sculpting metropolises? Honeypot ants fill their own sisters as food silos. How much less they take than humans — having exoskeletons, harvesting honeydew. But suppose they were the same size and had the same inventive capacity to make weapons of mass destruction.

Iraq, ant colony the size of Canada — completely dismantled. No schools. No street safety. No public health. No licensing. No clean water. No steady food source. No pay for anyone who worked for government. And THEY are importing slaves again. 12,000 Bantu from Kenya to Arizona.

Sugar Museum | On the docks, United Grain Growers' block of silos snorts and gasps, sucks and blows its blue ducts. Then sugar mountain between grain silos and fish wharf — *it was necessary to wage continuous war on rats,* company history notes — a rodent doomsday book starting in 1930. One worker ran a trap line. 5,396 rats plus 3,053 mice bagged as of 1958.

PR unlocks sugar museum door, flicks on fluorescent lights to panoramas of beet and cane fields. Impatient: *why should a historical society be involved, it's a private company?*

Spider webs drape handwritten original proposal on Hotel Vancouver letterhead. An 1890s minute book is fading: "... we have been caught with a considerable stock on a declining market...." Sugar crystals speckle glass display cabinets. Dust blankets iron sugar tools.

A cast-iron guillotine for severing three-foot cones. Metal rocket-shaped moulds. Iron kitchen tongs like welder's vice-grips. Long, toothed jaws of a crushing tool dropping ground-up sugar into a box shaped like a violin. Sugar axes (small tomahawks) for chopping at the tea table. All these made redundant by snowfalls, blizzards, avalanches of ready-to-use crystals. What only royalty could have in the 18th century, every housewife could buy in the 20th if she had cash, and she could work for cash in all sorts of sugar refineries. Bone char, still used PR says, beside Deeley & Co. door to a Char Dryer. Charred bones filter out impurities, then they're burned again to remove impurities, then used and burned till they're dust.

To leave whose remembrance of things past? Who owns history? Under glass in a model factory with rows of mullioned windows and huge chimney for fires boiling sugar. 1909: more brick and mullioned windows made a sugar warehouse on the CPR track. Human polyps secrete idea-reefs. Ugliest building in town, folks said. 1912: factory sprawled six storeys high, three city blocks long. Operating its 1910 space ships — the vacuum pans — bulgy, bolted sections — thick-edged portholes.

Careful control of temperature crystallizes tiny or quartz-size nostalgia.

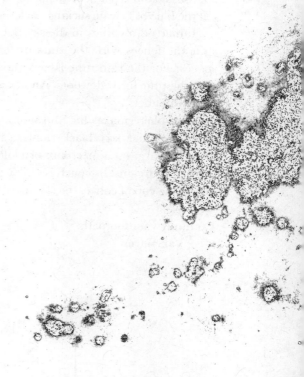

Sir,

I am gigantic magnet crowded with tiny domains. They are bent. They are riveted. They are welded in violent mechanical sacrifice, till their antenna return to their tails. For the vessel deviates according to the magnetic heading of its building ways. Or the strength of coercivity applied in the current system of obedience. Where are the poles, in their secular drift when spring begins in Aries, Pisces, Aquarius?

In long periods of moorage, the shift is gradual. Rapid realignment comes with launching or when the vessel fires its guns. The shells of utterance collide and letters scatter, defying grammatical lines, but always circle back to what they cannot say. So polar bears see constellations neither rise nor set. The red iron of Public pulls out the blue of Private sucking back the Public red.

Humans draw lines in the sky but the sky moves — do they shift the fences with the stars or leave them circling empty spaces? For the ram time is now the fish time, the fish time is now the time for water pots. And there is no velocity of escape from alphabets.

Atmosphere makes life and utterance and twilight. Without atmosphere the sky is black, rainless, silent. Sun burns and night freezes. The gas station croons of a killed poet and the sleeper on the bench dreams. So much is visible in cities, and so much hidden in the cup of coffee, the silk scarf, the calla lily.

Faithfully your footpath,
Geo, Vancouver

Cartographer at Work sails the 20th Century grid — no longer trees, but streets named Chestnut. Cypress. Arbutus. Maple. Beside the tax authority, the macro-brewery, the flags and the ever-burning flame in Seaforth Peace Park, Cartographer boards the Knight bus — Robert Knight (1829–1913) claiming fame for owning property in South Vancouver. The word roars off over the Burrard Bridge, on a route of its own: Harry Knight, a BC photographer, preferred soft-focus pictorial moodiness; John Knight, Captain RN, fought in the American Revolution with Vancouver's man, Captain Broughton, then got his name on the Kwakwaka'wakw inlet where thousands of the first people fished for eulachon. The Knights of Labor in the 1880s elected Vancouver's second mayor, lobbied for a shorter work-day, tried to stop the import of low-paid Asian workers. The word roars on through the Meccano-set girders of the bridge: a feudal tenant trained for mounted combat; a man devoted to the service of a woman; a horse-head chess-piece that moves in L-shaped leaps. *By sea and land we prosper,* says the city motto on the bridge house — a logger and a seaman hold up the city coat of arms.

On the bus, people gaze with bussed-eyes through steamed-up, rain-splattered windows. There's a sudden reek of disinfectant as a man walks down the aisle. Wipers idiotically, hypnotically sweep and stop, sweep and stop. People read. Hold their heads up. Wet walkers get on. Ball-cap guys with not much work and a few days beard. Death by Chocolate, touts a passing store. Wet people slump in seats, or smear fog off the windows — trying to see out of the Knight bus, while Cartographer records latitude and longitude for land, sea and air, and wonders whether *The Amphibians* (of BC) could be like *The Bostonians* (of Boston) or *The White Oaks of Jalna.*

Night Bus | A man wearing a wet blue wind-breaker over a pink "hoodie" falls into the next seat. His forehead shows little hair. His hands are large, pudgy.

HOODIE: You a journalist.

CARTOGRAPHER: No — a writer.

HOODIE: What kinda writing?

CARTOGRAPHER: A poet (this seeming somehow definite — final, plus Cartographer has found people seem less threatened by the term, as in harmless flake).

HOODIE: What do you write about?

CARTOGRAPHER: About the city — I'm collecting material on the city.

His face is moonish, the lips heavy, the eyes blue.

HOODIE: You got some books out?

CARTOGRAPHER: Yeah.

HOODIE: What was the title of your last book?

CARTOGRAPHER: *A Thousand Mornings.*

HOODIE: You write whimsical poems?

CARTOGRAPHER: I've been called philosophical [pause, but what would that mean to anyone, so add to explain] — as opposed to anecdotal.

HOODIE: What's that — anecdotal?

CARTOGRAPHER: Telling stories about people and animals.

HOODIE: It's better to write than do nothing.

CARTOGRAPHER (thinking, It's better to swim than to sink; better to piss than get off the pot; better to stitch in time than stitch nine): Yeah, probably is.

HOODIE: TV's nothing — not even there, really. TV can be fattening — you sit down, watch TV with a bowl of nachos — I don't watch TV.

CARTOGRAPHER: So, what do you do — do you write?
HOODIE: Naw! I don't have the golden pen you might say.
CARTOGRAPHER: So, what do you do?
HOODIE: I'm unemployed.

Unfolded — *Little lamb, who made thee* — imply, like employ, means enfold.

Not enfolded means not being used profitably; having no job for remuneration; uninvested. Without clothing.

HOODIE: I do temp work here and there.
CARTOGRAPHER: What kinda work?
HOODIE: Cleaning up construction sites. I had one job where I had to lay turf down. They brought all these pallets of rolls of turf and I laid them out side by side to make a lawn.

Architects should put light switches beside windows, Ponge wrote, so you could switch off daylight and contemplate the night.

Sir,

The most beautiful order of the world is still a random gathering of things. My siblings, Venus and Mars in the galaxy. The heart in the body, its human hinges open to felt compartments.

What closets. What operates their sluice-gates beyond gloves and boots, coffee and cigarettes, the *Odyssey* or *Arabian Nights*. Swinging from disrepute to archangel. Merde to chocolate. Passé to vogue. Driving driving driving on, ever on, with dithyrambs. Will it be too expensive to feed children. Can we afford to have forests. Round and round in a hundred thousand world-lets. Reality's category error. Orbiting a phantom called Reason.

The surface layer of my thought's a thin shell of air — only seven miles thick — a cerebral cortex, the bark of the brain with little tendency for adjacent air masses to mix. Pressure rises on the Motor Front sharply discontinuous with pressure of the Sensory.

What does the brain know of the blood. Or the heart's seasons. Hidalgo the hidden zings and warps asteroid gravities, then spins a loop from Venus to Saturn. Hearts rampage. Humans, raccoons, rats, viruses swarm beyond saying. My trees, drunk on CO_2, grow faster and faster. My ice melts for more clouds to keep out scorching Money. The ever-expanding rush through the phase called Life. Languages of solar orbits spinning their own stars in most beautiful orders of worlds.

Your astralogue and faithful agent,
Geo, Vancouver

Department Store | He wanted the next-

door farmer's daughter. Married her the following Wednesday. He wanted holidays. No more seeding machines; no more harrowing. Apprenticed with a merchant, $200 a year. He wanted to meet the public: a salesman. A tight-buttoned black suit, high collar, a bow tie. A new line to bring three times the profit. He wanted land growing corn ten feet high. Bought 200 acres of Manitoulin Island. Thousands of rocks under the snow. A baby every two years. A plank cabin with no plaster, wife and four kids. A log trading post, then a two-storey frame store on High Street. Bad cheques and bad suppliers. He wanted not to be bankrupt. He sold tobacco: 4¢ a plug, 45¢ a pound. Sold sugar and tea and butter and jam. The finest assortment. Cash only. A full range of Winceys, Cottons, Flannels, Tweeds, Lustres, Ladies' Clouds. Scythes, Snaths and Cradles. Everything for Teaming and Livery. Crockery, Glassware and Harvest Tools. Syrups, Dried Apples and Raisins. Men's long boots, one to four dollars. Women's laced boots from a dollar. He paid off loans; wife and kids crowded over store, whatever cabin he could nab. Carloads of oxen for Manitoba. Red River flooded; busting Brandon real estate. He sold posts and ties, grain and furs. Beef carcasses. Dressed hogs for the mills. Bought two more stores. Had a bad manager and $30,000 debt. Wanted to be magistrate. Store burnt down, someone he'd convicted. He bought land 3000 miles west in Vancouver. Wife coughing blood and pregnant. He took eight kids in the Colonist car. Took a loan of $7000. Built a three-storey store on Westminster Avenue. Sold boots, shoes, groceries, men's clothes. Wife, ninth child, and eldest daughter dead of consumption.

Buy on the Avenue, he said, *We sell everything.* The road to New Westminster of mountains and forest, named after old Westminster of Whitehall and Big Ben. *Buy on the Avenue.* He put boys at school gates handing out ads: boots 75¢, caps 15¢. Bought job-lots of silks, fur muffs, collarettes, capes. Some goatskin. What you don't know won't hurt you. He went into drygoods, the very latest shawls, blankets, ribbons, yarn, hosiery. *Experienced managers in every department.* He wanted a million. He wanted the finest drug business in Vancouver. Apprenticed son Jack — a qualified druggist at 19. Vancouver jammed with gold rush. He moved the family over the store, rented out the house. Jack coughing. He bought up hardware, snowshoes, sleighs, clothes, dog harnesses — everything except dogs and he knew where you could get them. Jack worked the drug counter; raised his brothers and sisters; gave tickets to school kids for free drinks at the soda fountain; stayed up till wee hours packaging candy in little union jacks. Jack 25 died of consumption.

Another son in sales and a daughter in bookkeeping. The youngest delivered orders by handcart after school. He joined a jeweller, and a china merchant. Saw a cheap lot going on Hastings (the mill street), frogs and skunk cabbage eight feet below sidewalk. Borrowed $79,000 from the Canada Permanent Loan Company. Used non-union labour. Said he was a working man's store. Strung loop-lights across the street, hired a four-piece orchestra Saturday nights. Sold the Westminster store and house for cash, bought out partners. Added two more floors. Two more sons. Took a house in the posh West End. Took a second wife. Took a thousand acres of Kentish farmland, gave them up. Bought the store next door. Bought a ranch in southern California. Dabbled in walnuts and roses. Got elected MLA. Died alone in an easy chair, dreaming of 25-cent-days.

Proclamation ı Captain Vancouver stands before City Hall's stepped '30s megalith — wig, top-coat, breeches and bird-splatters — scroll-chart in one hand, the other raised shoulder-height and pointing for days, years, maybe centuries spell-bound north by northeast to imaginary passage.

His right index finger pointing out to the east block and parking garage (just racks for two dozen bicycles in 1900). Finger pointing to avenues and condo towers set in bluey dioramas of coastal mountains.

All a dream in 1887 — the City a scene of primitive disorder (to one King's Counsel). Three hundred and fifty signatures prayed to City fathers for a playground. Men rowed out to Brockton Point with Surveyor Hamilton. Then back to black stumps and crumpled branches at Bute (King George's favorite prime minister) Street, clambering over branches, boulders and felled trunks to the line on the map called Granville.

There's a block you can have — Hamilton waved at a profusion of humps and hollows — in the distance a few wooden houses, Westminster Avenue and beyond that the mudflats. Workmen did the rough clearing, then cricketers went over it with picks and shovels and rakes. Made pitches of coconut matting. Cricket. Football. Baseball. Balls stuck where they landed in the soggy ground — caught up like the men in games — their magic swings and shouts, their enchanted revolutions in knotted tapestry — stakes in forgotten history.

The grounds caught too — named for Cambie (chief of the trains from Yellowhead Pass to Burrard Inlet). Grounds for Al Larwill's cabin, devoting his life to boys' soccer, lacrosse, baseball, the games of clean living and telling the truth. Forgotten Larwill Park paved over and leased by City to bus depot, post office, army, movie-maker rigs.

Sir,

Life eats things. So do wind and rain. And black holes. Life eats sunlight, eats sunlight-eaters, eats life-eaters. It could have stopped with sunlight. It could have stopped with sulphur from the ocean vents. But it began clumping into algae, trilobites, lungfish, coral, brachiopods, shell-crushing sharks, seed ferns, monkey puzzles, butterflies, palms, brontosauri, titanic birds, mastodons. It made a moby dreaming.

Cells became bodies. Cells became livers, stomachs, brains. Cells organized and divided labour. They colonized. With roads and telephone lines for free amoebae. Cells ooze gibberellins to make seedlings foolish. The stomach of cells is the world. When the food is gone, cells shoot cyclic hormones from their backsides, like drumbeats. They head for the squirts, they swarm into cities, erecting their bodies in towers.

Which is the one and which the many? A person or a species? A word or a language? A body, 85-hundred years old, covers a thousand football fields. Or a body is amoebic. One is a fruiting body or one is hungry. One is a passenger pigeon, or a bead on a wire — an ant-leg on a page, a bit in a byte. Erupting tornadoes of spores.

Can spores make laws? To have only so many spores, to have only so much stomach. Can spores make laws to see gravity with the eyes of elephants, spiders, daffodils?

Ever mycelial,
Geo, Vancouver

DISCOVERY AT SEA | 6 |

A Street Is Territory Borrowed1

A street is territory borrowed from the past into which we engulf ourselves in search of transfiguration (Etel Adnan). Immersion in a mural on Commercial Drive — pointy evergreens, turquoise lakes, beige rocks, Athenian colonnades. *The most enormous cathedrals emit an amorphous crowd of ants,* Ponge said, wishing humans would build shells closer to body size.

Idle Ant orders tomato and lentil soup with mustard oil and a slab of oregano bread. Building stalagmites of word drippings in a café on the head drive. An altered state of consciousness, Benjamin said: tourism, like someone on hashish. Watching bus-boys with tubs of dishes. Watching lips on hips of hot pink skirt — waitressing.

How to find trust in a world of personal gain. Friends suddenly saying the Chinese peasant girl is better off in a factory, where she dies at 18 exhausted. Anything else today, sir (pink skirt, high falsetto). Friends suddenly saying we can't afford lo-cost housing (though we could 20 years ago), forgetting about tax cuts and ethics of lo-wage factories.

How to find trust. On the Drive, Beckwoman's and Dr. Vigari's hang out their shingles. A squeegie girl hangs out her midriff and miniskirt, halter top and chains — doing a windshield — a guy's mud-splattered pick-up. She reaches over muscle wheels, gets smeared with dirt, then races to the other side, does the mirror, catches a coin as the light changes, and the cars rush around her. Ants of industry — ants of idleness: what does a city think it's doing?

At Lord Seymour's School, eleven-year-olds charge around carrying plush toys (what the peasant girl died making). One with a dog rushes at one with an octopus, barking. Across the street, by the potentillas at the mouth of the footbridge, a man lies back in a red Camaro, closes eyes in the sun, a woman's head bobbing rhythmically at his crotch.

Men at Earl's Industries, too, are hard at work. Spraying acetone. Buzzing saws. Chucking i-beams in the barn. They're building angle-brackets, carrying rebar, torch-cutting steel. Flipping switches to Earl's Twin 20 us Patent. The machine flexes its hydraulics, sliding its thorax and pelvis in, out, in, out. Arms, legs pointing skyward flap up and down. A giant ant on its back.

Central Executive I Earl of Granville and King George's crossroad — people mill about — in working memory, which has slave systems, the Brain Book says — phonological loops for shopping lists, and little scratch-pads for sketches. Mark the hotdog stand. Mark the Corinthian columns of department store etched in cream terra cotta, lifting up its classic mouldings and grand balustrade along the roof. Mark the giant logo-topped, hard, white bank-tower on its launching pad. Le Corbusier's architext of pure calculation: Vancouver Centre. With marble facing and London Drugs. Show-car parked out front. Muscle man flexing blue tattoos on his biceps.

On the upper floor, women with sunken eyes (you see them cleaning buildings at night) buy a bag of chips or a bottle of pop. Or a microwave oven, a magazine, some peanuts, a birthday or get-well card, a chocolate bar, vial of perfume, saucepan, Tupperware, lotto ticket. Down the moving stairs for computers, cameras, TVs, boom boxes. At the clerk's desk, a streetman in threadbare jeans fiddles with a digital camera, hands shaking. Pushing buttons this way and that — muttering, Just got it, don't know how it works.

Memories take months, even years, to form, the Brain Book says — in the hippocampus, a horse field — in Greek it's the horse monster of the sea, though it looks like a wishbone. Humans become feral after nine months on the street. Animals make memories in dreaming. Of French buildings. Of following three men in pinstripes discussing jackets, trousers and vests. You can't put brown with blue or blue with tweed. Of course you can, there's brown and blue in the tweed. We're torn from the same cloth. But the squares don't match the printed lines.

And the elevator has no buttons for other floors, though the lobby's illuminated by 256 light bulbs and weather information for passersby.

X People | Walk down Keefer Street, thru Chinatown, past Columbia, to motorcycle cops and police cars — people in red vests with yellow x's. Sidestep them into Sun Yat-Sen Gardens' animal paths through black bamboo, tall stalks waving overhead. Peninsulas jut into lily-pads and pond-sky dotted in round leaves.

Out the main gate, the bust of Dr. Sun Yat-Sen. Sun Zhongshan in China — National Father. His three principles: Mínzú, Mínquán and Mínsheng, Wikipedia says. People's Connection, People's Power, People's Livelihood: food, clothes, houses, right to land, freedom to move.

Don't go along Keefer Street (x person). *They're filming a stunt.* Cars line up on Carrall, honk, turn around, go back the other way. Rats in a maze scoot up Suzhou Alley between old-folks home and the old silk shop. To Shanghai Alley and the great bronze bell from Guangshou, the Yong bell (Han Dynasty 200 BC), marking the passage of local-borns Mow Wo, Moy Hoy Fong, Nun Yeung Toy, On Chong and hundreds of others from Chinese to western ways. Then across a parking lot to Tinseltown tower with its twelve movie theatres. Lots of x people and cops and a couple of red tanker trucks: the rainmakers.

Sun Yat-Sen gathered exiles in British Hong Kong. Attempted a coup in 1895. Failed. Went to Europe, Canada, the US, raising money to bankroll uprisings. In 1911, the Qing emperor fell — 2000 years of imperial rule over, kaput. Sun Yat-Sen the first president.

Around the corner comes a crowd of people and contraptions

all hitched to the same chassis. A truck towing a car. People wearing helmets. A woman primly holding motorcycle chrome. Then the camera crew. Police and x people wearing little mikes and earphones. The tow operation halts beside dilapidated trailers of abandoned construction site. People adjust masses of sleek hair. Wait.

A girl in 6-inch platforms climbs the steps from Keefer to Beatty — what movie is she acting in? — black sling-backs, chrome studs across toes. Fishnet stockings. Pink skirt with hot kisses on buttocks. Strawberries all over her spaghetti-strap top, her salmon-coloured hair gelled up from shaved scalp like a rack of lamb.

A hungry rat first explores the site. For without memory you cannot know time or place. Cannot think a future. Rat brain gives each gate, each corner, each passage a memory neuron. Scientist watches computer picture: memory neurons firing theta waves. Same waves as rats dreaming.

Movies too shot off and on location's imaginary places.

Sir,

The universe is expanding. I cannot go back to labyrinthodonts. Tooth-writing my sediments. Shale, sandstone, yanked thin by mountains drifting west, grinding under tectonic plates. I cannot go back to Silurian conodonts, Paleocene creodonts, the tree-toothed, the bright-toothed, the nail-toothed, the humped-, crested-, breasted-, the mill-toothed mylodons, the leaf-toothed sharks, the squalid-toothed whales, the mixotoxodons, the hypsilophodons, the loxolophodons, the ungulate-rodent-carnivore tillodonts, the socket-toothed thecodonts, or the tooth-writing ants who ringed their gates with molars from thousands of tiny mammals.

The universe is expanding. Pangaea cracked to Laurasia, Gondwanaland. Continents repatched with cranial sutures holding time, possibility, laws, beliefs, growing apart again. Like fingernails and hair. Simply going on when Chicxulub blackened continents. The ferns came back in centuries. Millennia for cleansing ice. Life simply going on. Turtles, hellbenders, mudpuppies in aquatic muck. Cat-eyed burrowing toads puffing to walking balloons. Becoming Hades' proto-guard-dog, the Human's mousy mammalian ancestor, then the condylarths — leopards with hooves, seed-eaters, leaf-eaters, meat-eaters — 50 new genera, hundreds of new species every million years — proto-sheep, -pigs, -horses, -rhinos, -tapirs. The tree-born, bumpy-toothed squirrels, 200-pound shrews, rabbit-sized bears with columnar eyes, cow-sized hedgehogs, four-ton uintatheres. Six-foot, hatchet-beaked birds with hands instead of wings. Pignosed turtles. Greenland merged with Canada and Scandinavia. Then unmerged. The north sea at 28 degrees. Then California down to 9. Twenty-one hundred cubic kilometres of volcanic ash covering Nevada and Utah, and then again 25 million years later, three meters thick in Nebraska. Killing a herd of rhino at their water hole, grass seeds in their throats.

10 million years later, humans reading this. Finding the 3-toed gomphotheres, the Miocene camels, oreodonts, protoceratids, horse genera doubling every 5 million years, some with claws. The pronghorns — who still run at 100 klicks; whose mothers swallow feces and urine of fawns, no scent of young — for barbourofelis whose teeth stab and cut, but do not chew. Humans finding mastodons and mammoths, humans thinking Clovis people killed them. Clovis people then disappearing with other animals.

Did Clovis people choose? Did hunters of bison and passenger pigeons? Those who ate cod? Drive cars. Use fridges. Flush toilets. Live on stocks.

The universe is expanding

stupidly
Geo, Vancouver

We make what we are here for

Corner of Hastings (Vancouver mill) and Hawks (John Francis, 1890s stockholder, Coal Harbour land syndicate). Astoria Hotel parking lot — the Sheway Community Project trailer-hut. A She, in shiny lo-slung pants, drifts past the door, fingering her spaghetti strap — top hanging down below bra hooks. She shuffles back and forth for the passing cars, thighs pinched together as though she doesn't want them to part. Another She at the bus stop, bulldog body, all black and leather — jacket studded and flapping, crooked-cut leather skirt — black boots. Black thick socks. Sooty matted hair.

We make what we are here for. But who is We? and what was here before?

Do you say Kee or Kway, asks the bus-driver / Us-driver, long white braid curling round his shoulder. *Sure, three bucks'll get you the Seabus to Lonsdale.* Arthur Heywood L, held the mortgage on Moodyville Mill. Foreclosure got him a chunk of waterfront city. Fond of prize-fighting, he refereed a match at Hart's Opera House, before Wilde's Marquis of Queensbury. Is it hugging or wrestling? Pugilism or boxing?

Seabus to saws, ships, docks, loading, unloading, grain, planks, steely containers. Blue sheds belt yellow hills of sulfur. Cranes and ramps clamber at mountains of sawdust. Black freighter lounges in the sea before a city blocked, cubed, terraced out of mountainous green. The Pacrose of Nassau, red stack, orange lifeboats. Yellow cranes and container-brackets ladder its superstructure. Seabus to barge of soggy woodchips. Seabus to tree-trunk pilings, and booms of logs. *This little wooden world,* said Captain Jack Aubrey, Master and Commander ... *the proposed training ship "The City of Vancouver."* Saturday we'll have a street collection in aid of her — *the Vancouver World, 1910: a Flag Day.*

Tractor tires guard the bows of spanking red and white tugs. Beyond them, empty roof rafters and wall studs frame the sky, skeletons of old Burrard drydocks. Shipbuilding gone. History repeats. Clearing land for condos, marinas, cafés, postcards, T-shirts. Lonsdale Kway / Kee Market's giant barnacle, cruise-ship / cruise-shop, feeding on the human tides flushing in / out the seabus terminal.

A pipe-smoking wooden sea-captain in a dory decorates the tug shop. Plus the stock totem-pole: a bear wearing a salmon like a bow tie, just west of the old Moodyville Mill and a slough the Squamish called Uthkyme, meaning serpent pond. *We had a teacher at the school named McMillan and he whipped the Indian boys unmercifully* (the Archivist recorded Mrs. Alice Crakanthorp in 1936). *He would go out in the bush and cut a switch and whip them with it. The Indian boys showed their resentment by draping an apple tree in his garden with dead snakes. When the tree was shaken the snakes began to wriggle and drop to the ground.*

A Piece of Cake I

Lunch with J—, far from the jolly food fair of the Market, with its plastic plates and forks and paper cups of pop. Here's a glass case with occasional sandwiches and a dozen cakes in slathery icing. Armchairs and fireplace. Students studying computer books. Young salespeople and consultants meeting their clients. To Lonsdale Antiques, says a sign across the lane. Animals in top hats and bulgy waistcoats march along the signboard — rabbits, geese and frogs, followed by Mr. and Mrs. Pig, who are asleep.

What does she mean by restless metonymy? J—'s mouth twists to one side, lower lip pulling left to protrude, in luscious perplexity. Lyn Hejinian's "Strangeness" — an explorer's journal: *"there it is," "there it is," "there it is" ... restores realness to things in the world.* A piece of cake. A poem. A dream of a van camped beside

Lake Superior. Driven away by three hillbillies to their shack of magazines, cans of beans, dead couches, three-legged tables, and rusty mirrors.

Give me back my van now, and there's no questions asked. Okay. Take it. Drive it down the front steps. Excuse me, ma'am. The dream-van's going down these steps. Excuse me. But the teacher asks what's the most important element? The van stops, no one speaks. She runs her finger down the periodic table: most important is function. Her her she her, chants a velvet sombrero — John Cage singing *Mureau*. Teacher, feeling copper and radium, disappears and the dream-van carries on down the front steps of the shack of the hillbillies. It was a piece of cake.

Sir,

Humans long to be the one to erect categories. Categories have sex with reasons in 69 causes. They choose presidents and philosophers. They decide who to kill and how to sell. Categories are better than raccoons. They are completely modern. Their walls are mere skins which are light and weightless, their lines strictly governed by ethics of style. How neatly their functional cubes fit into the sky the red bacteria of a blood cell, its hundred and twenty days running 75,000 trips streets, alleys, lanes, cul-de-sacs, lungs to muscles — oxygen out, CO_2 back. The white cells, made in marrow, migrate to thymus, a bunch of thyme at the breast-bone giving them homing notes for liver, heart, guts or kidney. Cells reach out a solitary foot, pull themselves after it, squeeze through walls, engulf bacteria, viruses, cutting chunks off invaders, showing badges to their mates who make fingerprints binding the strangers. Cells remember words for 10 million fingerprints.

Spermtails of bulls, whales and ginkgo trees, antennules of lobsters, cilia in lungs, spores of water-mold, the rods and cones of the human eye all wired with telephone dials from spirochetes. Mitochondria and ribosomes speeding along cytoplasmic phone lines. The whole shebang marking, figuring, coding, scripting the living tissue of thought. The whole shebang tunnelled for signalling, channelled for passage.

North
by northwest,
Geo, Vancouver

DISCOVERY AT SEA | 8 |

Scarecrow **I** Crows prefer life in towns and cities. Their noses full of feathers — their eyes intelligent and hazel-brown. On battle grounds, they eat the dead. They eat the corpses of plagues. They are wise; they are wary; their plumage jet with a violet violent sheen; their feet ebony. Charles II welcomed them to the Tower of London. And the executioner called his block ravenstone.

A fledgling lands on the porch. It starts up into the white wall as if it were sky, and into the green door as if it were trees. Bashed back by this solid sky and forest, it dashes everywhere but the empty space where the steps go down to open air. Anything but that empty space below the nest in human heads, that nothing, nothing, nothing but falling. A broom nudges it down under a privet bush; it holds out its wings, whispering squawky gasps while the parents zoom down and try to lead it upwards. Flapping to the street, it lands near a truck tire. Cars whiz by.

Then on the Economist's porch it holds its beak open, emitting small wheezes. Marmalade the cat paces back and forth on the other side of the glass.

The Economist steps out in pajamas, with coffee and stock listings: armies of numbers marching across newsprint. Oil is up. Language is down. Religion, up. Compassion, down. Appearances, up. Stake-holders, down. Up is up. Down is down.

You've got a young crow.

What should I do?

Are crows up, down or flat?

Marmalade bats the fledgling, a toy stake-holder, and scampers along behind, big birds diving at him, driving him into some bushes. Tattered fledgling dashes for porch. Cat chases it into the railings. Fledgling squeezes through, falling down between human houses.

I'm going to phone the Centre for Disease Control, the Economist says, *In modernity we require only what is functional.*

Thai Palace

Thai Palace | A Toronto writer comes, like a wise-man from the east — to read in Vancouver. But first the inner circle will dine with him at the Thai Palace. A little trip to Prathes Thai, kingdom of the free. They'll meet an emerald Buddha, some teak-bearing elephants, seladang, gibbons and flying-foxes, not to mention gondolas of bread-fruit, damar oil, sirih and salak crowding the canals of the floating market. King Ramkamhaeng who made the Siamese alphabet may be receiving. Or King Rama, founder of Bangkok. Or the poet King Narai, who ordered Pra Maharajkru, Pra Horatibodi, and Sriprachya to compose verses in the Klong and the Kap — so Thai children could learn Thai things instead of Jesuit things.

They'll meet the princess beloved by a crocodile or the princess given away before birth to a yak, her mother exchanging her for her favorite fruit. They'll glimpse Krung Thep, City of Angels, Phu Ping Palace at Chiang Mai, or Wat Arun, the temple of dawn. They'll attend Kathina and watch the king offer robes at the end of vassa. They'll see Mount Inthanon and the rich rice fields of Chao Phraya river, the fabled Khorat Plateau with its cattle, horses, pigs, cotton, peanuts, corn and hemp. They'll buy freshly mined rubies and sapphires. And shiploads of tin just in from bucket chains and jigging tables, gravel pumps sucking ancient river slurry, running it through baffled palongs. They'll meet a shaman or a hunter with his blow-gun. Or a wild Wa collecting human skulls to bring himself good health and crops.

Among the gold lions, glass dragons, and elongated cats, beers and martinis are ordered. Peanut sauce discussed. And the department store that used to make Vancouver's very own peanut butter, empty for 10 years except for pigeons and squatters charged with trespassing. City in a stew, whether to make it 400 condos, with a hundred tossed to the poor. A union organizer mentions 2000 food and cleaning workers fired from hospitals will not be hired back, even at low wages. They're "tainted." Peanuts gone bad. Like Anna Goodman on KPFA asking Bill Clinton about Shell Oil and 90s greed. And he saying, Look, you're not supposed to be interviewing me!

In Thailand, unions and strikes are forbidden, says Microsoft Encarta.

The palace guard in their black and white uniforms with brass buttons arrive, carrying bowls of rice, curried beef, prawns with noodles and chicken in peanut sauce.

Sir,

Be advised, as Don Quixote said (after knocking down a Bene-
dictine friar he thought was a magician and then losing half
his armour and an ear to a page who chased him off) *this ad-*
venture, and any like it are not island adventures, but crossroads
adventures.

No island here. No governorships with simple metaphors. The
opposite of an island is a marsh. A bog. A swamp. A morass. Lucky
horseshoe islands always off in the distance suddenly lurch up
and lunge like angry windmills. Freedom and democracy, free-
dom and democracy, they scream waving their arms and killing
everyone in their path.

Sir, Be advised of the ground you stand on. Sun'ahk. Kum-
kumalay. Smumchoos. Sundew, cloudberry, sphagnum. Little
Mountain. Lost Lagoon. Freedom. Democracy. The properness
of Property. This is Mukwaam. Your foot is sinking.

Sir, Be advised, Life does not explain. God is geophagic, and
the square root of philosophy is sin and opinion. Seize the means
of windmills, if you like, but they will still wave their arms.

Sir, Be advised, you cannot see where the visor has no holes.
And, moreover, you have no VISA that's interesting a savings ac-
count near paradise.

Geomantically,
Geo, Vancouver

Fireground I Four-alarm blaze, in the artists'
studios above the old ballroom and Miss T's Cabaret.
Cooking popcorn on a hot-plate (rumour rages 'round the
crowd) — popcorn? — yeah popcorn — at 9 AM — yeah. Who eats
popcorn for breakfast? It was seeds popping for hash. The oil
caught fire. Burned arms and legs. Firemen got her out on a ladder.

10:30 — the roof's evaporated. Window frames (once swivel-
ling on their centres) open their charred sashes to smoke-billow-
ing sky, above black shattered beams and smouldering shards of
lath and plaster. The air stinks of scorched rubber. Smoke pours
from a room with a computer monitor on a desk. Below it the
abandoned sandwich-boards of the Internet Cafe and Pender
Grocery. Melted rubble, charred paper, burnt cans and bottles
litter the street.

Water jets fill the block with clouds of droplets, and rattle sheet-
ing dangling from the parapet.

Flames lick up a stairwell, threatening the Victoria Block with
its facade of double pediments and scrolly medallions. Young
men from the Backpacker's Hostel, bedrolls and boots on hefty
packs, sit on the sidewalk looking back at its window sign —
Double $35, Single $25 — smoke swirls around its red brick, its
green wooden facings that dream of classical pillars and denti-
lated cornices.

Fire is sharp; water is dull. The somnambulant coolness of rea-
son overtakes the cutting torch of sense. News crew opens black
suitcase of mikes, lenses and wiring, sets up portable stage-lights
and camera on tripods, loads video cassette, clenches camera grip
and swings it round to film reporter with jets of water and smoke.
Snow-white CBC van with flying saucer on its roof screams News
World up to the satellites. Community in Crisis says Salvation
Army van dishing out sandwich packs and bottled water.

Everything at the scene is heroic: navy-blue men with badges
and photo ID, a leaking coupling spraying furiously, folds of hose

jumbled between trash skips, POLICE making hand signals, trucks bracing on pavement, men climbing ladders, men in yellow bunker gear and red helmets, men in white in clustered confabs, men tossing water-bottles to buddies, men in sky-buckets against looming thunderclouds, men speaking to walkie-talkies, yellow do-not-cross tape tying up lamp posts, jacket saying clothing wagon, chic suit talking to firefighter outside Wow Interiors, Ladder Truck No. 1 backing up, patrol shooing off watchers sneaking under yellow tape, postie holding up camera getting permission to go in, water bouncing off computer at Internet Cafe, firemen lying on street with rows of oxygen tanks, hats, rubber suits, men with tanks and sticks emerging on roof of Victoria Block, then bringing back shiny galvanized trash can to bystander. Bystander reaching inside, and lifting out his bumpy, foot-long lizard — a hero — a bearded dragon.

Melt House 1 Sugar-factory museum offers wall-sized dioramas. Cane fields. Beet fields. Black field-worker in ragged grubby clothes — no front teeth. Black cane-cutter, stubby machete in hand, in a field log-jammed with hacked stalks. Ozama Mill, Santo Domingo — Columbus planted sugar here in the 1490s. White manager, clean, immaculate, among 10-foot grasses — beautiful plumes waving in the wind.

The *Ingenio — Primum Mobile* of the plantation. Slaves drove cattle harnessed to poles round and round its rollers. Others fed in stalks. Rollers catching fingers dragged in the whole man. Hatchet ready to cut off an arm. Dark brown juice pouring down to cisterns for boiling.

1770: sugar islands took 13,000 a year. King Charles' Royal African Company had the monopoly (buy for £3, sell for £16). No matter how many slaves, planters wanted more and cheaper.

1938 women on crude wooden stools, among factory chutes,

piles of sacks, reels of thread, fill gunnies on conveyor belts with pure cane sugar, stitching them shut on clunky machines. White bonnets, like 18th-century milkmaids.

Her numbered brass tag daily in the Time Office. Payday: her tag at the Pay Office for an envelope of cash. 1924: sugar factory paid $800,000 dividends. Ladies pay envelope, 1932: $14.00 for 40 hours.

When a slave wife became pregnant she was exempted from flogging until after delivery. Two weeks later she went back to the fields. Eleven hours a day, six days a week. And home to her hut of sticks and cane trash, with its sleeping mat, pot and calabash gourd cut into bowls and spoons.

Sweetlands | The ants. Honeypot caste-workers hang by their claws, in the hundreds from a vaulted roof, storing nectar in their social stomachs. Warrior Aztecs lap honeydew from mealybugs before heading for battle.

Heaven planted us to please. Ourselves. Sweetly wrapped in quintessence. Life is sweet. Light is sweet. Peas, summer, sleep and Jesus are butterscotch. Home sweet home. Sweet lollipop smell of success. What's rapturous and divine if not sweet in star-spangled heaven?

Barbados classed Negroes not as chattels but as real estate, part of the ground that grew the sugar cane, the ground that ran the crushers and boiled the syrup.

The stock of molasses on hand continued to grow until storage facilities, first barrels and later tanks, being taxed to their limit, the excess was run into the inlet, says refinery history. Slower than black-strap in January, molasses oozed sticky fingers, past barnacly pilings, through saw-mill trash and sunken boat skeletons, into the sea. Until everything that had been the sea, the wild outside, the unclosed, the place where anyone could wander, was filled with dark stickiness.

Coal came in scows men unloaded in barrows. To fire kilns, melting 80,000 pounds every two days and filling the air with thick black smoke. The factory whistle with its mournful roaring sigh of a large entangled animal still calls workers 6AM, 6:30, 7:00, 7:30, letting them go at 11:30, 12:00, 3:30, 4:00. Prolix liquor cascaded on elevators of men climbing to the lips of vats. On catwalks, in splattered overalls, they stirred barrels of blood, fresh or otherwise, with baseball bats and hurled them into steaming tanks. Clotting it bubbling to the surface, the blow-ups. Sugarfactory 1988 consumed enough bones charcoaled to fill 45 three-storey filters. Defecating sugar.

1868: Canadians ate 15 pounds a year; 1890: 44 pounds; 2002: 86 pounds.

What brave estates! How bravely the canes grow and the negroes goe tumbling down the trees.

Sir,

Nothing goes faster than the speed of light. Except bolts of thought for centuries unravelling. Or not. Thought forgotten wavelets wiggling out past Menkar and Deneb. Nose of a whale, tail of a hen. Draw lines in the sky, to perch on with Cheshire smiles. Flip, flop, hang by a claw in dark energy. Two billion with less than $1 a day.

Thought seeks thought. Or not. Thought tangles into giant thinking: telescopic, microscopic proboscides. Unstoppable. Six billion mouths. Progressed beyond all previous epochs of human mouths. Flow-through in the brain that's thinking everything. Whizzing thoughts around in words' infinite flavours of quarks. Or names of beavers.

What do we know besides hunger and the uses of hunger? Humans build nests as birds do, make concerts in the way of cicadas and frogs, and damn up rivers à la *Castor canadensis*. Listen to the tail-slap on the pond, the whistling and buzzing of gravity, dark repulsive gravity pushing the universe apart, dark matter bending the paths of stars. Climb beyond trails, tracks and shadows, beyond trial by peril. To foresight and the scaffold of use.

Outside these, only care — find some way to care.

From my iron core and granite eggshell,
Geo, Vancouver

DISCOVERY AT SEA |10|

Bird Books ı Eagles in the park emit long piercing shrieks as crows dive-bomb them. Below their perch, fluffs of cottony seeds puff over the old race track and Cottonwood Gardens' higgledy-piggledy plots of blackberry tangle, dog roses, planks around a tree, rows of beets, carrots, lettuce, onions. A rat dashes into a lavender bush. Bald eagles, the Bird Book says, eat mainly dead or dying fish.

Later, Mr. and Mrs. Eagle perch on a branch, while baby eaglets in their crotch of sticks busily grow wings, and make beaks, claws, and fabulous feathers from meals of dead or dying meat. A man and a woman arrive with their poodles, and boast. I knew a guy up the coast who found a baby eagle and he took it back to the house and it ate his socks. I knew a guy who shot an eagle and the next day five eagles shat all over his car. I knew a guy who threw squirrels up in the air and the eagles'd catch them by their tails. The Bird Book says eagles eat fish. That's a laugh — get another bird book. Have a look through binoculars. Things seem farther away than they are.

Bird City ı Cloud Cuckooland, Aristophanes called it. Frank Lloyd Wright said the modern city was a place for banking and prostitution. Little else. He made prairie houses interior flows, Spartan walls, low, shingle roofs hovering on lawns. Domestic axes riveted in stone hearths. Birth of suburban ranchers and split-levels.

Erasmus said the city was a huge monastery. A city consists in men and not in walls or ships (Nicias). *Towered cities please us then, And the busy hum of men* (Milton). The Germans thought the city a social agency — a mastermind of colonies, armies, broods and bunches; a masterpiece of pods, flocks and litters. The city is an immense tumultuous shipyard, said Futurists. A rigging of rented pretenses shuffling the dreamed-of.

The city is an Ellesmere Island beaver-pond 5 million years old, damming streams with freshly chewed sticks. The city is a million cave swiftlets talking clicks, eating two tons a day of insects. The city is the bowerbirds' avenues, galleries, maypoles. They build boudoirs. They decorate them with green moss, red berries, silver shells and blue plastic. They steal their neighbours' porches and gingerbread and even the living rooms till they settle their pecking order. How does the bowerbird know how he stands, the scientist asks. How do humans know how the bowerbirds know?

The city is ant hill, fish hatchery, mould patch. Taking shape from form, the legible forgets what it's never seen. Universities build millennial time machines — invisible walls capturing light and air under concrete roofs. But knowledge will no longer be this solidly built thing that sets out a ship for all time. In that other university, that other time machine, the hatchling homo eaglet raises a woolly head from guano and sticks, totters around, then disappears again in its nest.

Queen Dreams

Queen Dreams | Her majesty comes to the city, gracious and noble and happy and glorious, longing to reign over us. Her ministries of consumer affairs. Sniggling in and out of pockets with the moose and bears, the beavers, loons and bluenoses. Wearing George IV roses, shamrocks, thistles or her lover's-knot tiara. The queen. Slipping in and out of wallets in Queen Mary's Girls and her wreath of flowers (Nizam of Hyderabad gave her the diamonds; the rubies came from each and every one of the Burmese people).

Lie back and think of the queen longing to reign maple leaves. Perched in white satin with a red-lipped smile, above the rolled map and the blackboard in gradually fading school-room paint. Blue sash across her shoulder, elbow-length white gloves, hands carefully clasped just below the belly. Is that the Russian fringe on her head, or a puffy white hat? Prince Philip's beside her, white gloves in hand, medals on his chest and hat under his arm, *his* crown jewels well tucked away.

Lick the queen. Lick the Lahore diamond and floret earrings. Lick the queen in 1959, in her blue velvet cape and Order of the Garter star. Lick the queen beside the Parliamentary library. Lick the queen for thirty-seven cents. Lick her when she's 76 in front of a maple leaf. Lick her in the legislatures. In the ministry of health, the ministry of finance, the ministry of environment, foreign affairs, defence, customs and immigration. And in the courtrooms of the city, lie back and think of the queen pursuing the accused. The queen that defends our laws and ever gives us cause.

Sir,

I look back through curtains of shimmering names. Goose-tansy.
Silverweed. Tormentil. Bloodroot. Fivefinger. Cinquefoil — the
many-clefted, the snowy, the creeping, the louse-like, the three-
toothed, the twin-forked, the swamp-lover, the springing-forth.
Hanging by strings from Potentilla who came from the Potentil-
leae who came from the Sanpotina who came from the Roper-
culina who came from the Rosoids in the noble lineage of Roses
in the class Magnoliopsida in the phalanx Spermatophyta in the
supertribe Tracheobionta in the kingdom of Plants.

I look back at a curtain of divergences, forking and branch-
ing and forking and branching, where the Greek *posis* begat *pos-
sidere* (to sit on property) who begat dispossession and madness,
the nephews of *despot*. And Latin *pot* begat *potis* (the master), and
his brother *potens,* who begat potent, potentate, omnipotent, the
cousins of *possum* who said I can, and *posse* (the sheriff and depu-
ties), who begat *pouvoir* (tasting peppery), who begat puissance and
power. And *posse* (the power of the country) begat possibility.

Fingers fiddle the strings. Snipping, patching, jigging the
shimmering names. So the strawberries beget ladies' mantles,
and the potentilla beget strawberries, and the dusky horkelia
are cousins to little potences from Norway. Strawberry dwarfs
spawn erect dwarfs, the cousins of many-branching potentates
and three times removed from swampy despots.

Sir, I look back through buzzes, hums, whines, ribbits, barks,
yaps, snarls, roars, woofs, purrs, hisses, meows, bleats, bellows,
oinks, squeals, neighs, whickers, nickers, brays. Chirps, cheeps,
peeps, tweets, twitters, warbles, chatters, squeaks, hoots, whoops,

crows, coos, honks, quacks, clucks, squawks. I look back through
language, to lips, teeth, tongues and throats —

in constant divergence, deviance, splitting,
swerving, wandering away, parting and departing
Geo, Vancouver

Scaffolding ⏐ Plato's Necessity holds a rainbow pillar buttressing the heavens. A great whorl within which seven other whorls slowly spin the other way, each one carrying a singing Siren and the Fates: Clotho, Lachesis and Atropos. The spinner, the giver of lots, the shears on the thread of life — these are the daughters of Necessity.

Here, in human scaffolding, the courthouse: an imaginary arena. From Roman senators weighing a case of treason, in the torchlight of the Curia. Or the centumviri judging thieves and frauds in Basilica Julia — its vaulted ceilings and clerestory windows 100 feet above palatial chambers. In the courtrooms of modernism, the law is low, flat, rectilinear, with model trees.

The courthouse steps — they settled on the courthouse steps, built a cabin — fan out in concrete slabs up a pyramid anthill of registries and chambers, ending mid-sentence at a wall, water rushing over it —no Roman columns — just a 10-foot wall of justness — pediments and scroll-top columns gone to the art-gallery — a glass roof, an arcade, an atrium over its low flat concrete. Glass on metal scaffold over the hush of carpeting, potted plants, blind-folded Themis. French *escafe,* a shell; Latin *scapha,* a light boat, a skiff; Greek *skaphe,* a trough. Anne Boleyn on the scaffold took the fatal stroke.

Outside the courthouse, a woman with crutch scoops water for her windshield squeegie with globalized burger-joint paper cups. A teen in lo-slung jeans coolly tilts her buttocks as she drifts up Howe Street. Live to Love, says the Celine / Dior trapeze-woman swinging out from a billboard.

Inside the courts, the buzzing of innumerable bees: If your Ladyship, Lordship would turn to page nine hundred and fifty of the transcript. My friend and I have reached an agreement, subject to your Ladyship, Lordship's approval. I'm afraid I must ask your Ladyship, Lordship for an adjournment to review the sixteen binders of new evidence. Objection, M'Lady, M'Lord, my friend has asked a leading question. A moment please, M'Lady,

M'Lord. If it would please M'Lady, M'Lord to refer to Exhibit A. I believe, M'Lady, M'Lord, it's under tab 100w of binder 12c. Those are all my questions, M'Lady, M'Lord.

Her Majesty Versus Murdock 1

Order in Court. All stand — the lawyers in their black gowns, behind their brass bar, the Accused in his box, the jury in their box, the sheriffs of the Accused and the jury. The oak-panelled room fills with shuffles and plumps. All sit. His Lordship in red mantle and red-cuffed robes swivels his chair to address the jury in their plaid shirts, angora sweaters and track jackets: *I am the judge of the law,* he says, *You are the judge of the facts.*

Made from Latin *facere.* Facts make fashion statements. Ache about like general factotums, and quarrel in factions. Make difficulties with facility. Cook up features, defeats, fetishes. In them dwell the gods of raccoons and humans. Facts are erotic.

Proof beyond reasonable doubt, His Lordship continues, *Mr. Murdock has no obligation to prove he's innocent. Be cautious in discussing the case. Later you'll find it difficult to change your mind.*

To doublets, doughnuts, douches or doubts. Double thinks or double flats. The facts make reason's rations and ratio's rashers. Outside the ratio, all is obiter dictum. For *logic,* as Nietzsche said, *rests upon presuppositions to which nothing in the real world corresponds.*

The Crown charges Mr. Murdock robbed Mr. Mack, assaulting him with a weapon — namely a hockey stick. Crown must prove Mr. Murdock took property and used a weapon with force to hit his victim.

Through the lot lines of words, not boundaries of worlds, propriety becomes private and peculiar. But who, or what is public? *Homo laborans* slaves away, making more *homo laborans. Homo faber* produces more and more products, the way facts make artifacts and factories make faculties.

Only testimony of witnesses is evidence.

Sir,

I set out for Point Unexpected. The passage was windy. Humans had a propensity for tribalism, poetry and cunning. They were like a lot of little things breeding furiously and operated by chemicals. My boat swerved in all directions. Its course was radiant. Humans were not radiant; they thought they knew what was animal; they took logic for granted, and believed in causes, likeness and categories.

Philosophy and wisdom were missing and presumed dead. Language had drowned. Humans thought History had ended. They loved the triumph of sugar. They could bite and count like machines. Yet they built skyrises and trade-webs like birds and spiders. They loved to climb, exceed and outdo, yet they shadowed, traced and stalked. For the grails of knowledge conform to crusades of sense in their fixed constellations. The Nature that is positive. The Wealth that is money.

I came to the Strait of Outcries and the island of Utopia. Discovery was a cover-up, recovering the couch of the boatswain. Yet things were reflective. Space and time were sensitive, warped with gravity.

Sir, I must catch the world in its blood, and climb the rigging of understanding. I am explorer, implorer. I seek Experience, Nous — imagination's crossroads of body and language, a kaleidoscope that displays appearances, unravels functions, builds architectures.

Ever roadless,
Geo, Vancouver

DISCOVERY AT SEA | 12 |

Brain Coral

Brain Coral **|** Words themselves are insensible, skeletal cups. It's tongue that has sense, darting out its feathery tentacles into night.

A clutter of bindings and dust-jackets presses against glass storefront. Shelves sag. Volumes project every which way into the room. Hundreds of tomes piled or toppling or ranged in rows, spines up along the floor. Rising like a flood around shelves that loom to remote ceilings. Book sniffers slip their antennae down the remaining crevices into History, Geography, Art, Physics, Biology. Philosophy or First Nations. Heads tilted sideways reading the spines, sniffing through R, S, T, sniffing out *The Innocent Traveller* by Ethel Wilson — not Fiction A – Z but Canadian Fiction. *Or it might be over in the office* — a room distantly budded with all the most sniffable books in another branch of the coral brain.

The English woman is on guard at central command, an oak desk hidden in ramparts of dusty-edged pages. Around her, display cases and counters slumber under heaps of cloth bindings and disintegrating paperbacks. Several minions hold outposts keeping an eye on sniffers and gold-embossed covers. The street door opens and the owner comes in from the office, charging down the path to central command — his mind on estate sales and catalogues, collections of World War II memorabilia, 1920s art-deco typedesign, or the writings of F.R. Scott. He topples a mountain of books nearly burying a sniffer. Engages in hurried negotiations at central command. *So what's the total damage?* He's packing boxes. *$4000.* Sniffer writing cheque.

Suddenly minions and English woman vanish. *I let them go for coffee.* He talks briskly, abstractedly, eyes shifting here, there, on sniffers in their cracks and crevices. His brain's disappearing down the track, he's got to get there — another collection of all the most foul and wonderful aromas — it's gone on sale to the first to identify them all — Limburger cheese, lilac cologne, marzipan cookies — he's got to find money, got to outsniff the sniffers.

S iwash Rock I

The world's in hungry plates — a Eurasian plate, an African plate, an Arabian plate, a Caribbean plate. A North American plate, grinding relentlessly westward. Forcing Juan de Fuca's plate down to molten magma. Disgorged in volcanic dikes, cooling to a core of basalt that splits the sandstone at Siwash Rock. Words too erupt, crystallize, fracture. Forming rifts and faults, jostlings of clastics, isolated outcrops.

S'i'lix, the Stó:lō called it. The Squamish word whites spell Sl'kheylish. Slahkayulsh, said Chief Khahtsahlano — *he is standing up*. A seastack with headdress of scrub fir, standing in the waves, face to the west. Near a brass plate "In memory of Robert Dennis Tribe, age 17, of North Vancouver who at 3:15 PM Sunday, June 5, 1966 failed to notice it was low tide...."

You'd have to go east about a mile off Siwash Rock to see the old potlatch house, Chief Khahtsahlano told the Archivist. *First narrows — you'd think it was a big bay and Siwash Rock a sharp point.* Vancouver missed things rowing past Pookcha, the floating whale back, or Khapkhepayum, the cedar place.

1860s, they called it Nine Pin Rock, head and shoulders a manikin for bowling balls.

Mother was telling me, Miss Crakanthorp said, they never called the Indians Siwash unless they were disgusted with them. Mrs. Eihu remembers her grandmother at Kanaka Ranch *talked English, had small feet and always wore boots, and a hat. Try and do like the whiteman does, she would say — copy him — don't be like a Siwash.*

Siwash had a wife, about eighty feet from Siwash Rock, Chief Khahtsahlano remembers, *a rock, sharp shape. Like woman's got peak hat, it's got mouth and eyes.* The Archivist drew two headstones on watery lines, for graves in his sketch book, the small one Siwash Rock's second wife, Sunz.

He didn't have two wives (Chief Khahtsahlano). *Sunz. Chunz. Chants — a big sandstone rock covered with water at high tide*

(Andrew Qoichetahl of the Squamish Council) — *Chants is Siwash Rock's fishing line rolled into a ball — also a big hole in the cliff where he kept fishing tackle and did his cooking.*

"Dear Sir, You published on March 13 an illustration of a Totem from the West Coast of British Columbia. But why is it described as the work of Siwash Indians? During my residence among these Indians I was never able to locate any tribe by that name. If a Coast Indian was called Siwash he resented it as much as any coloured person would resent being called Nigger" (the Rev. F.S. Spackman, Vicar of Marple, Cheshire, formerly Principal of the Indian Residential Schools, Alert Bay).

When whitemans call me Siwash I say Go to Hell (the Archivist recorded Chillahminst; working in Hastings Sawmill the day Vancouver burned). *Siwash Rock was once an Indian man. I think one man make the world, but some people say three men. They go out sturgeon bank, out Point Grey. They wash themselves, wash themselves, wash themselves, make themselves very clean; keep themselves very clean. They get very powerful. The three great men go all around the world making it. If they find poor people, they give them stuff so they no more poor; teach them how to do things better; show them how to get food; but if they find people too smart, too clever, they say, You go to hell, we not trouble about you. That's how Siwash Rock came to be where he is; he too smart, three great men turn him into rock so people see not much good to be too smart.*

To kill stupid cleverness. Is it necessary. Or wait for plague, drought, greenhouse to eat humans.

Siwash Rock, the guidebook says, a Vancouver landmark located in Stanley Park.

" .... This plaque erected by Bob's friends as a reminder of the danger of diving from Siwash Rock."

Canada Day I In nations of sense, what could human mean to ant? Godzilla, the human meteor — the big collapse of ant universe. Or the human bulldozer: smoothing new ground for creature colonies — 20 million acres of southern North America to the sovereign fire ants, *Solenopsis invicta,* after humans cleared forests for beef and dairy farms.

Ant nation; human nation. What could human mean to whale? to cougar? What could Canada mean to Pangaea? Terra incognita, once-upon-a-time land of dinosaurs and tree ferns, millions of shifting niches for panoplies of life. Humans thinking whales, ants, ferns have boundaries too. Yes, but not nations. Not notions of lines printed and pressed into paper. Humans declare war on fire ants. *Invicta* invective. Ants ooze venom, humans spray Heptachor from army aircraft.

Thought's rhizomes echolocate rhymes. Writer-ant tunnelling for seeds, insects, small vertebrates. For the schemes of things. Ants and eagles bear eggs and humans sometimes break out of shells, preoccupied with ruins and fragments. Dreaming steel silos for souls (one egg-layer; ten-thousand workers). Sending ant-hills' crinkly sound-waves ever outward, in ever-expanding dream-bazaars of exploding universe.

Sir,

I seek block-and-tackle purchase for my conception. The journey onward, ahead, elsewhere, out and out and out — absent, away, unconscious, banned, impossible. You hero the spaceship of history, you hero philosophy, the moons of realism. I collapse in forms casting for concrete and rebar certainties. My crystalline mantle de-finites its molten core — pressed, pulled, sheared and twisted. I wake to empty plywood sheeting. Floating aromas of a moby dream.

What of rich dirt and poor dirt — drit dreet detrital — left at the roadside, humanity's dirty-dishes factory for drunks dirtbags dirt-dobbers. Scratching deserts. So garden soilers get the pay dirt. How much will they pay? For their dirty work at the crossroads, their computer pie-charts, before a long dirty sleep eating their gods. Loon, bear, moose, beaver — so many nickels and dimes. Even leaves made into pennies. You are exchange. Message-massage. Swapping utility's clear-cuts, clearance sales, your duty to clear customs, balance cheques — be clear, operate blind as a figment. Blind as convenience. A telephone pole.

My ground moves muddy turbid pitchy. To jam the circuitry. Beep bop glitch songs thatched signals.

Pyroxene, olivine, garnet,
Geo, Vancouver

Fire Engine **|** Burning House, the brain book calls itself — a crowd of fireflies racing through axons to dendrites, leaping synaptic junctions, swirling up gleeful astrocytes — the star cells — brilliantly streaming proteins, ions of calcium imagination. To memory's dreams and passageways. To myriad connectivities. Rapid persistent chemical change. Continuous oxidation of photons, air wavelets, anthracite verbiage, releasing light, heat, ideas.

Get on like a house on fire. Misfire and hang fire. Fire questions or stones. Make irons in the fire. Do a fire box or a fire drill. Fire engines' yanky crankshafts. Cease fire, get fired. Sit on a fire-escape, chat by the fireside. Swilling firewater by the light of the fireworm.

Humans build alarm codes' steel doors, unburnable beams' exit signs. Humans underwrite shingles kindling tinderboxes. Talk up risks for premiums. Make acts of man Promethean. Before Christ, Egyptians built water pumps. Roman Vigiles shot squirt-tanks in Londinium. Forgotten by the Dark Ages. Humans made bedposters with gooseneck nozzles. Bucket brigades to fill them, six or eight men on the brakes. Every house must own buckets and ladders by law, every house supply volunteers. Carters paid a shilling. Set fires to get money. Leather hose cracked and froze. Insurance magnates doled out spring-loaded ladders. Steam-pumps like coffee-pots stoked with coal. Cloth hoses rolled on wood-spoked reels.

Cities burn. Brain cities burn. History a seething language of possibilities. The ground 10 feet thick in felled trees. In black bowlers, the real estate men stroll your phantom streets. 1886. Sunday, June 13. W.H. Gallagher, Esquire volunteered three men in the AM to beat back the CPR slash fires. Went home, had lunch. Three men never seen again. Wind blew a coal hulk a mile down the shore, blew up the sky in a flaming tornado melting a hundred buildings — and the single tolling bell at St James church — in 20 minutes. Humans, so many higgledy-piggledy ants scattering, dashing from street to street, feet burning on fiery boardwalks, running for the sea, wading into waves, carrying payroll money, account books, a sewing machine, a crate of dynamite — Sunday school teacher with just his bible — up to their necks. Gasping at scorching air. Only three bodies afterwards decipherable, their faces livid, suffocated, a man, wife and daughter who jumped down a well. Five weeks later clapboard parapets slapped up again, squaring off the streets before their peaked roofs. Engine going full-roar. Wagon heaps of lumber and men in bowlers rolling down roads to saloons and trading posts. Between the east-end forest and the west-end forest.

A sphyxiation ı *It often happens,* says Hume, *that after we have lived a considerable time in any city, however at first it might be disagreeable to us, yet as we become familiar with the streets and buildings, the aversion diminishes by degrees, and at last changes into the opposite passion.* For sun avenue and moon alley, fire highway and water cul-de-sac, hotel knife and flesh cloister, château dry and wet yard, public drive and household rooms, hunter boulevard and gatherer lane, piazza ploughshare and ground wynd, sacred parade and occult walk, above circus and below gardens, villa day and night asylum, cutter mansion and weaver mews, master auditorium and servant bungalow, order capital and chaos ghetto, father castle and mother kiosk.

The human condition is one of habitat. Habitude. Habit hutches. Arsonists, mesmerized by lapsing disassemblage, abstract in-co-therence, hope at last to lose facade. But fire-fighters bring attack hose and aerial ladders. Piss their master-streams on this oxidation, piss 500 gallons a minute. Who gets to piss higher? They crank open hydrants and flake out yellow hoses to save the farm-iseum. Save the internet café, the Pender Grocery with its smoking ice-cream sign. Save the retro-girl fashion-boutique and the haberdashery for the finest ranch mink.

Percivals and Galahads and Lancelots in yellow rubber chain-mail charge up on their red steeds. They lower their visors and dash their swords at magician flashover and sorcerer bankdown, driving lances into false doors of habitation. Doors that are not doors. Doors that lead endlessly to the same frames. The knights are the frames and the frames are crusades for the doors, the video-tape of cameramen, the microphones of news crews touting avenues and lanes, boulevards and alleys. Far far away from the manholes to metropolan unconscious.

A Theory of Fire

Theory of Fire **|** *As is evident to all, fire and earth and water and air are bodies. And every sort of body possesses volume, and every volume must necessarily be bounded by surfaces* (Plato).

In sleeping bodies are moby dreams of the not-seen, the not-allowed, and the wet noses of seeing-eye dogs, the dream-seeing metaphors. Anything becoming visible casts its shadowy moby dream.

Wonderful fire brigades. They marched with hose reels in Dominion Day parade. 2000 feet of hose for water tanks at Maple Tree Square and Dunsmuir and Granville. They had meetings once a week. They had a minute book. They had a firemen's minstrel show. They got a spring-loaded aerial ladder and an engine pulled by horses, with a boiler of burnished nickel. They called it M.A. MacLean after the mayor.

So far, neither ambulances nor fire-engines carry ads for pizza, real-estate agents or cell-phones. Just a motto, Serving with pride. Since 1886. Wandering as musicians, gleemen, jongleurs, bards, troubadours — they buzz and hum of hydrants and halls, codes and trucks — red, yellow or white. All over North America, the words in their songbooks — fuel, oxygen, heat, combustion — form the sides of a pyramid.

Let it be agreed, then, both according to strict reason and according to probability, that the pyramid is the solid which is the element and seed of fire. Consider the fineness of the sides and the sharpness of the angles and the smallness of the particles and the swiftness of the motion — all this makes fire violent and sharp so it cuts whatever it meets.

Sir,

The geography of out there is not the geography of here. I stand on Archimedes' lever waiting for him to jump off the teeter totter, hallucinating rationality, while I seek a geo-logic — strangely divine it through dark teeming mirrors of chattering signals, ideologies. Throw aside ego and mastery, yet set a course — still find navigator and ocean. How romantic, you say. But I say there's no neutral Archimedean point — what's your bias, oh rationo-classico-anti-romantic? What technologies of destruction lurk in your graphomotors? What shadows mark your measurements? Are you taker or trader? And if taker, how differ from gobbling mould or ants? And if trader what's left uncommodified?

To co-modify. Patrolling walls, look across them to forbidden grounds. Become the grounds on which you stand, that stand under your standing. Research their plains, cordilleras, lakes, tundras. Stub your toes. Bump along on the wordscape. Skim over boxes of money and slavery. Remember somewhere before slave cities. Lurch back, split into forks, zoom into, pull through, stall, prowl, straggle, pose in formation. Sniff the tracks of a moby dream — super-orgasmic nation of urges exigencies wishes itches lusts — untamable, unreckoning, yet compelled, hurtled, driven by megalopolic brain, heart, stomach, lungs. Bursting my seams, bursting the seaming of things, before the big collapse. So laugh. Read omens. Make fictions, objects, dogmas, manifestos — to speak not for all, not for ever but for just this photon buzzing along through the whatever — to speak of a logos — a writing rewriting ever rewriting hummocks / potholes / edges situations — possible fingerings —

geognosical
Geo, Vancouver

DISCOVERY AT SEA |14|

Lovely Drive **I** The City raises its totem coat of arms, heralding its dreams: a tall ship, some felled logs, a choo-choo engine with cowcatcher sweeping the tracks, balanced round the axis and spreading branches of a Douglas fir. Incorporated AD 1886. *By sea and land we prosper.* A city of fishing and hewing. But the City has nightmares.

The City writes itself over, with bearded men, one holding an axe and limbed tree, the other a paddle and net; the two supporting (like lions and unicorns) a shield of wavy lines and winged caduceus, *the axis mundi* / wand of Mercury, main highway between heaven and earth of west-coast forest. Two snakes curl about it: fire and water, sulphur and quicksilver, tying / untying waking and sleeping — this herald's power, this transcendence.

Wish fulfillment tops the pole with a knight's helmet (place of hidden thoughts), tops the helmet with castle battlements — a walled medieval town. The whole phallic tower topped again with a sail and mast waving a flittery pennant.

Dream on, oh City, a third time, for the College of Heralds, London England, suppressing hacked tree-trunk and primitive paddle, compressing logger and fisherman to clean-cheeked boy-scouts proudly flanking waves and dogwood flowers. Each with a hand on the shield, a well-beloved horse, while holding in the other his axe or net. Displacing, subverting what libidinal histories — wrapping the knight's helmet in lambrequins' feathery feminine banners, and launching the whole mobile contraption with a Kwakiutl thunderbird cleaving the waves. Sea and land not enough: the City takes air, too, to bellow its prosperity, its pro hopefulness, in a Queen's armorial bearings.

The last chief Khahtsahlano remembered the first order of City business: claiming a military reserve (his Squamish homeland) for a giant park, a giant memoir of perished forest. *It being of more than local importance* (or exportance), the City called on Lord CPR Strathcona to name said park, and *he* named it for Governor General Lord Stanley of Preston, who went down in history for a hockey trophy.

September 27, 1888. Lord Stanley not present. It was Thursday. A procession to open the Park formed on Powell's street (17 years Superintendent of Indian Affairs, invented for his charges industrial boarding schools). Then down Cordova, 46th Viceroy of Mexico. Down Lord Granville's Street, along King George's Street, across the bridge over the lagoon, and around Lovely Drive to Chaythoos, home of the last Chief, where his father Khaytulk and grandfather Chief Haatsalahnough were buried. Mayor Oppenheimer standing beside Khaytulk's tomb, a little house (glass windows, red blankets) raised on poles where Khaytulk lay in a canoe, Mayor Oppenheimer dedicating the park to Lord Stanley.

Khaytulk built a barn there for cows and horses. And a house covered in cedar shingles (Chief Haatsalahnough's house stood there before it), Corporal Turner of the Royal Engineers marking it on his survey map, 1863. *We was eating in our house,* the Archivist records the last chief, *Someone make a noise outside; chop our house. Surveyors come along and they chop the corner of our house. My sister ask whiteman what he's doing that for. The man say, "We're surveying the road." My sister ask him, "Whose road?"*

The road came, it knocked down the house. Squamish having lived there from time immemorial. Cutting a tree to make a canoe, they'd found a mask inside. They'd called the place Whoi Whoi (masks). They'd scattered clouds of eiderdown before the British boats of George Vancouver. At Whoi Whoi, they left acres of white-roasted shells and the bones of ancestors, a midden, eight feet deep, a thousand years old. Dug up, spread on the road — the Lovely Drive.

The Architect

I They build three-lane highways through the jungle, workers carrying leaves on their heads. At the gates the soldiers frisk them. They build fenestrated domes with breezeways to galleries and vaults. Cities seven million strong. Foragers gather leaves. Shredders cut them up. Pellet-makers feed tablets to swelling mounds of food tended by weeders and harvesters. Cleaners spray antibiotics; take rubbish to the middens.

Seven castes — birthing, nursing, grooming, excavating, scouting, guarding, attacking, sowing, reaping — a thinking, swirling brain, each neuron a separate body with head, arms, legs — a language of scents — work parties chattering in camphor, civet, vetiver, patchouli, spikenard, durian, musk, eucalyptus, coffee, marjoram. More eggs for the Queen's breakfast, more pellet makers, more galleries, tunnels, rooms. The architect, whirled in a vortex, an absent centre. The architect turns — spindles on a lathe — hunters into warriors, farmers into armies, chieftains into kings with palaces, granaries, temples, agoras — chattering of Anubis, the jackal-headed patron of Cynopolis; Atum, the sun-god patron of Heliopolis; Bastet, the cat-goddess of Bubastis; Horus, the falcon god of Behdet; Khnum, the ram-headed guardian of Elephantine; Khonsu, the moon-god of Thebes; Min the erect-penis god of Coptos; Montu, the hawk-headed of Hermonthis; Neith the goddess of Sais; Nekhbet, the vulture-goddess of El-Kab; Ptah, the bull-god of Memphis; and Thot, the ibis-headed of Hermupolis. God-word electricity. Babeling an absent story, a moby dream.

The architect drafts a host of kings, managers, foremen, cooks, scribes, 100,000 peasants cutting columns, architraves, doorjambs, lintels, casing blocks; polishing stone, erecting ramps, dragging two-ton marble blocks, millions of them, up ramps, stairways to heaven — the first machines crafted of human bodies — now make zippers in Qiaotou, hundreds on wooden benches at vast work tables, fitting little tongues onto little sliders — all the long days

— rooms and rooms of them, Qiaotou shipping 2 million zippers a day, 80% of the world's market, for less than a penny a zip.

Brain as city, city as brain — in a leafcutter colony: three trillion neurons — thirty times more than a human. Why don't the slaves rebel? Why don't the trees challenge the forest? The salmon defy the sharks. The liver and heart flout the nerves. The skin cells deny the muscle. For cities without kings.

And he took the city and slew the people therein; and he beat down the city and sowed it with salt (Judges).

Babylon and its houses, from its foundation to its top, I destroyed, I devastated, I burned with fire. The wall and the outer wall, temples and gods, temple towers of brick and earth — as many as they were, I razed and dumped them into the Arahtu Canal. Through the midst of that city I dug canals, I flooded its site with water, and the very foundations I destroyed (Sennacherib).

Sir,

The Human sets out to apparent openings — awash in word-dreams, seas of dots and dashes, ribonucleic acids, Miss Manners semaphore. The Human unearths triangles and parabolas, molecules and quarks, ids and gravity. Roaming a vast inscripting of atomic weights and nuclear charges, the myriad genetic code in living things. Decoding it, recoding it in squiggles and bytes. Through coded doors are more and more, each door with its signs and cipher. Writing enormous messages — writing a voyage burgeoning, erupting, irrepressibly from darkness to darkness — beginning impossibly, going on perhaps another five billion years (in the current method of reading time), most of which without humans (bacteria have the longevity, floating their ocean cities), till the sun dies.

The longer the message the easier the code is to crack, but the script is endless. What does it mean without end, finish line, dénouement, purpose — what if there is none. With sample-case of handles, the Human discovers doors, goes through them, finds itself returned, grasping handle mid-air, to the same room in the same insect city — of means and ends, gods and kings. Where is the true door, oh humanus?

Door-maker dream-maker, resist the weather, beware the pleasant Tuesdays and Wednesdays, the little convenient markets of creamed corn, the ready-made taxonomies of sweet and sour, the lovely dioramas of wealthy elk.

With ears to keyholes,
Geo, Vancouver

DISCOVERY AT SEA |15|

The Straits of Streamline Moderne

The Straits of Streamline Moderne **I** Step through Williams' *Paterson* / the main entrance, brass / glass doors to lobby of City Hall, high gilded ceiling, banded chandeliers, striated pillars, striated trim circling the tops of pillars, streamlining the eye in parallel grooves of fluid light, over the marble wall and brass clock, the sign: Elevator, in Broadway type-face, zigzag frieze jig jogging along above the elevator doors.

In the elevator cab, more streams of striped marquetry run in stepped strips reframing frames in parallel frames of black and pale and dark woods. Then the Council Chamber basilica with clerestory windows, veneer panels, brass sconces, hidden lanterns — stripes and bandings on the chandeliers. City imagines itself in stacks of parallel lines like the layers of property owners Roman censors named: first class worth 100,000 asses, second class worth 75,000 asses, third class worth 50,000 asses, fourth class worth 25,000 asses, fifth class worth 11,000 asses.

The province of the poem is the world. I'm puzzled at the mace, a man says in the gallery, discussing when to say Your Worship or Your Honour. The gold crown gleams on its silver shaft, replicating, virus-like, the City of London's — with Royal Cipher and Arms of London, Arms of Vancouver and Canada's maple leaf. The Press are lined up at their desk, Managers of parks and streets in benches Reserved for City. Video camera poised. Two-o'clock gong. Men in suits (hi Dave; hello Larry) join the gallery, councillors arrive at their chairs in curved arcs Right and Left of Mayor, and a clerk rings a brass bell at the main door.

All rise. *Let the spirit of harmony and fairness prevail upon this assembly,* the Clerk prays, *as we listen to the many voices who so enrich our common home.* (Our common poem.) Clerk calls roll: You have a quorum Your Worship. Whereas … and whereas … and whereas … hereby declare July 8, 2003 Glen Edward Hillson day. He'd worked for AIDS sufferers, had died of AIDS. Was a renowned curler. His partner, family and friends receive the proclamation. Under fluorescent light tubes, particles of identical speed flowing free of turbulence.

Segway human transporter roams the halls of City Hall. Nuisance property must comply. Warn prospective buyers (ME *biggen, buggen*). I question mosquito control, Councillor, City authorized larvacide, not adulticide. Amendments for the noise by-law. (Buzz of automat transmitting automatically.) X Pizza, failed by-law, suspension continued. (X Pizza a hanging bridge or flying saucer.) Fees up, taxes up, Councillor, we're trying to get more out of business. Item four: complaint about suites-for-sale sign. Illegal, Councillor. But, Councillor, developer has converted (faithfully); he *must* be able to advertise.

Two clerks before the Mayor. Mace between them and gallery. *When the sun rises, it rises in the poem.* Home.

No Things but in Ideas

No Things but in Ideas ı Councillors sit in their chairs to the Right and Left of Mayor. In two curved rows, they are wings — of *États Généraux,* Paris 1789, the nobility: *aile droite.* The third estate that is most of the people is *gauche* of the king. A gold-crowned English mace on its belly — spectacular, from the gallery. The Right wing and the Left wing: where are they flying to? What streets aren't Reality? If you're the right real or the left real on the chariot.

Whereas the left is partisan and the right is non-partisan;

Whereas poverty is natural and money is noble;

Whereas the marketplace is the hand of God;

Therefore, be it resolved that the City is open for capital.

That permits are tortuous and taxes are grabs.

That no one should build houses for single parents, kids, disabled or elderly, especially not the City. And congratulations to the police for bringing order to the slums.

Trees and fees, says the Mayor, *how dear to citizens' hearts. I think that I shall never see a fee as lovely as a tree.* Or is it a levy as lovely as a profit, a wing as lovely as a lot value. I think, Councillor, that I shall never see a rent as lovely as a teacher, a lease as lovely as a hospital, a stock as lovely as a park, a mortgage as lovely as a street, a revenue as lovely as a watermain. A dividend as lovely as clean air.

Moved, that the City create just and sustainable access to nutrition.... Carried

Moved, that the City renew the former department store as low-cost housing.... Carried

Moved, that the City sell off the store to a private developer.... Lost

Notice of motion. Glide-lines on the heels of messengers, planes, trains. Whoosh of Streamline Moderne. Words' quicksilver channels zip through what's common: communicability's common. *Gauche, droit* in Castle City. The motion's on the floor.

Sir,

I am anchored in Quandary Sound. Anchored in the certainty of uncertainty. The straight thought of labyrinth. Language's moby dream feeding the machinery of trade so crucial to human dominance. I am lost / found in ants' neural cities. In every flowering coral brain's conception-dynasties I work / founder. I weld my vision. My clothes are despotic. My grammar conjugates antennae to senseless grammar. My cafés come from Atlantis, my cities from Utopia. Here is my palace of scarecrows.

Yet I turn around the sun. When the sun dies, I turn around what was the sun in the year 2003. Keeping a log, hour by hour, to be chronometer, compass-reading, a dead reckoning. To find nightmarks. Take a fix on Polaris. Find certainty in the cut of my sail against the wind.

Make way for celestial navigation. A north I am true to walking crab-like pulled magnetic in quaggy mirrorland. Yet lean into. Make way for Saturn, Jupiter, Venus, Mars. Cassiopeia. Make way for celestial bearings — something worthy of the heavens,

a system of buoys and a sea on which to float them,
Geo, Vancouver

DISCOVERY AT SEA |16|

Big News Café ⏐ Corner of Granville Street and Broadway with Kaplan Business College brick parapet, white neon letters scrawled on blue revolving sign. Sand brick with stone moulding and blue accents. Row of churchy pointed windows and brick piers modernism condemned. Not structural, so no right to appear with their peaked gables. Two enormous churchy-pointed arches over main entrance. Stone crests on either side, narrow twisted columns with scroll-top capitals dreaming of quadrangles at Oxford. QAT, DAT, SAT, PCAT, GMAT window signs. To Idle Ant in Big News café. Horoscope: *by all means help someone in dire need. Rush in like the knight in shining armour you've always wanted to be. But don't promise to bail them out unless you want them ringing you up morning, noon and night.*

Shining-armour Don Quixote Ant stares through café glass for big news — some Polaris or Cassiopeia for dead reckoning — haut shops on Lord Large-village street, Blenz Coffee under Business College. All merged in a big dream. Northeast corner, Royal Bank. Southwest corner, Chapters Books. Big boxes selling little cartons of fancy. *RSPs make all your retirement dreams come true.* The bank's yellow letters, black marble facing on concrete slabs and rows of aluminum windows.

City's a lot of going into — rooms — wombs. Non-city's one big space. In Shining-armour Ant-mind.

Defiance ⏐ To un-affiance. Unconfidate. At the hair-dressing salon, black swivel chairs, wall mirrors, magazines containing cockatoos. Walls of conditioners, gels, shampoos in rocket-shaped containers. The putting on of smocks, laying of heads in basins. Neck-breaking look at ceiling fans, wiring, pipes — water rushing cold warm cold through hair. Rubber-glove squeak. Donning of plastic sweltering tent.

Heavy snowfall of hairs sliding down. Snips. Buzz. Water spray. Jube-jubes' sour dragons on the counter. Hand-mirror held, chair whirled to look at back of head. D-i-f-i hair preparation rubbed in. Making hair stand up in spikes.

Is that Die-fie, like high fi, or Dee-fee like weewee?

Stylist with burnt orange swatch in forelock. Now into flying kites, having gone through bead jewellery, rollerblading, fishing and downhill skiing. Husband quit stock-broking; he now works in a lab testing mineral samples for gold.

It's defy, she says.

Sir,

Who are you? What are you? Racing your auto cars on my skin. Racing, erasing. Scooping me up to corral in your fences. Breeding my birds with broccoli, my fish with strawberries, my goats with spiders. Blocking my rivers. Slaughtering my forests. Drying up my lakes. Filling my lagoons with towerblocks and shipping docks.

Sir, you're burning burning burning. Your brain's on fire. With stadiums of sports teams, armies of oil drills, billions of plastic widgets and widget-makers, widget sellers, widget buyers, widget eaters, widget shitters. Dreaming of ever more wonderful widgets on the envy machines.

Gleaming gold Humanus, builder of pyramids, cathedrals, palaces, who are you? What are you? What are you standing on? What are your mud-blocks to a dinosaur, a sequoia, an ocean, a forest? What do you know, what can you say to match … hurricanes … tectonic upheavals. Why are you here

in the green fuse,
Geo, Vancouver

Public Safety requires clothes — a tunic, a livery, a yashmak — a sombrero, a pump, a moccasin — body's exteriors for flânerie's interiors. *Mesmerized by spectacle, the intoxicated rubberneck becomes empty, impersonal, public.*

Inside polished granite Safety, brochures offer rhymes revolving-rack: call 911 and help will come! Report Crime / On Line — to Police, the public face of the city. Make a Difference Every Day. In Captain Click's colouring book. Look left, look right, look left again. Before you cross the street. With the chickens.

Public Safety floor is brick-pattern vinyl. You can take polygraphs, clear records, pay fingerprint fees — $50 cash only — or push gently on Document Services — Person may be behind door. Okay, you're all done, you can go. Men in suits discuss marketing beside the brochure rack. Officers in shorts push through the gate from Property Room.

Backpacker looks lost. See the Vancouver Police Centennial Museum: the first drunkometer; large collections of badges, weapons, counterfeit currency; the Babes in the Woods Murder; Vancouver's intriguing history through the eyes of police.

The flâneur devotes himself to an ancient human dream — the labyrinth.

In the glass cage at the front-desk, a clerk drinks coffee. Another reads the yellow-pages. Racks of clipboards, a map of the city, a fire extinguisher hang on the wall. A large plastic plant sits in a corner. Welcome, says a sign, showing people in turbans and ethnic dresses. The backpacker tells his story: his car's gone missing: it was smashed into; he was staying at the Cambie Hostel; Busters towing don't have it.

A suit, bouncer size, with shiny black portfolio, approaches the glass. Then two Québécois girls in pink frilly tops need a police report for a stolen camera. Lost-car man paces back and forth past the brochure rack, on his cell to New York. Tony shakes hands with the girls, takes them upstairs. The police badge on the elevator doors splits as the doors open, reconnects as the doors shut.

A red sweater carries a garbage sack clinking tins up to the glass cage. On the other side, a clerk scans a computer screen. Red sweater: I gave them my wallet; they take it away. Tins clatter as he hoicks up the sack. Clerk in cage sorts through clip boards. How do you know it was stolen? It was gone this morning. When did you last have it? 11:30 last night. Where do you live? Salvation Army.

Dream House Centennial police museum. The old Coroner's Court. Roman-arched window and moulded lintel over the door. Inside, police are plugging jacks into a switchboard. No, just manikins at work. Upstairs chained off. No one's around, policing remembrance of police past. Yellow do-not-cross tape marks off chunks of masonry on the floor. Large hole gapes in the ceiling. Past cordoned area, man in blue on phone wants to get particulars. Around him, walls are full of boards full of fabled badges. Letters, newspapers, green garbage sacks litter 1940s metal desks.

DREAMER: Is this the museum?

MAN IN BLUE: It's upstairs.

DREAMER: 'Cuz I was going to say yellow tape looks mighty realistic.

MAN IN BLUE [walking into dreamer's face]: It's upstairs.

DREAMER [backing away from man in blue]: Upstairs is chained off.

MAN IN BLUE: She's gone for lunch.

DREAMER [back at door near sterilizer machine, vista into lab with large hooked taps, examining tables, institutional granite floor]: This is the old autopsy room where they cut up dead people.

MAN IN BLUE [pushing dreamer out the door]: It's a classroom now.

To study the death of Constable Paul Sanghera. January 7, 1982. Investigating a car slid off road in a snow storm. While reaching in to get papers, he was hit by a pick-up truck.

To contemplate Constable Bill Lindsay mounted on his horse, greeting a spotted fawn. To see a kit for making plaster casts of footprints, or look at the Harger drunkometer recording its first impaired driving conviction in 1953. A Deceptograph sports a paper roll and wiggly lines of lies. Sticky tape lifts fingerprints. Marked cards wear hair on the right side for aces, hair on the left for kings.

In the weapons room are gaff hooks, straight razors, throwing knives. Knives unfolding off a holster or retracting in a statue. A shiv hidden in a wooden handle. A half-scissor shiv, an ace of spades push-dagger. A bent-fork push-dagger. Death rings, key-chain switch-blades, throwing stars, tomahawks, belt-buckle knives — constant companions. Flick-knives, sidewinder switch-blades, pepper spray, mace, dart guns. The Morning Star flail with spiked balls. The chainsaw flail. Lipsmackers.

The coroner's courtroom — a barn of wooden beams and cross-bracing holding up a ceiling of white planks — fancies an old mead-hall or school dining room. Why are courtrooms windowless? As though the construction site within their walls must never remember a cloud or a tree.

In the morgue a bank of stainless steel fridges, bodies sliding head first or feet first. The autopsy room — gurneys and steel tables draining into sinks on white hex-tiles — boils in sun through a south-facing window. Perishing rubber tubes and metered vials hook up to large columns and jugs marked waste. A wall of formaldehyde body parts: hearts, ribs, fetuses. A spring scale hangs from the ceiling near a chalk-board tabulating results as you cut up the dream house, William Burroughs with babes in the woods.

Sir,

You are mute. I am mute. All that is written is written in flesh.— time recording itself in shells and chromosomes, cellular fractals — animal, vegetable, mineral. A game of 20 questions. No answering. Where species of words and organic speech greet miraculous living thoughts in sponge or fungus or Galápagos iguana. In time there are lines of articulation and lines of flight; lines of rupture and folds of membranes. Warped passage in resonant networks. Layered, pasted, woven passivities.

I am oxygen / iron / silicon / magnesium gravity imploding core. You are aquatically mute, yet skeletal speech. You make a type of machinity. Of symbols' mad clockwork, your rude designs to which you annex remote and hieroglyphic meaning. Yet my earliest bacteria live in the cells of your arms and legs.

And could explode in microbial tentacles. To break clock-work grammar. To dis-erupt. To un-evolve. To four-dimensional reckoning.

In Flatland,
whether you're a square or a circle, you look like a line,
Geo, Vancouver

Omnibus | *The omnibus seems to subdue and still all who approach it.... A calming, drowsy influence emanates from this ... machine, like that which sends marmots and turtles to sleep at the onset of winter.* Number 14 Hastings with ancient driver is virtually empty. Two guys don't get on. Don't know where their bus pass is. Sunshine, windy, hint of cloud as bus whizzes past the Brave Bulls House of Steaks, Canadian Tire's big red triangle, and the chicken plant steaming its evil fumes around trucks of caged birds, solidly walled from street and protesters. At the Serbian Orthodox Church, an elderly passenger reaches for a coin on the floor. Donut shop, A&W whiz past. Transistor-radio-blare and brake-screech from Capital Environmental Resource Inc., which is actually a garbage truck. Lease 1400 square feet, says corner-mall burger / dry-cleaner / family-restaurant combo, once a gas station. At the glittering flags of Trans Auto Sales, Capital Environment garbage roars into the lead.

Garden Drive: flowers of Blue Cross Pet Hospital, Martial Arts Supplies and Church's Chicken bloom. Animals are captivated by their food, philosophers argue, viz. a honey bee with abdomen removed will keep on sucking nectar forever. Humans likewise captivated by words, suck on their anthro logic. Blue panel-van: Magic Wand Carpet Cleaners noses ahead in the race to horizon's nectar. At Nanaimo Street, Sweet-Tooth Cafe, and Top Save Enterprise jostle for attention: we have thousand different kinds merchandise. Money Mart. Hastings Hardware. Dollar Island. One-stop mortgage (you'll never need another death-pledge). A mountain-biker rides up on the curb, then down between herds of cars. Passing Radio Shack, Bell Funeral Chapel, Tom & Jerry's Gourmet Castle. Death's another commodity. In the no-money-no-food machine.

Lord Renfrew's street and the Pacific National Exhibition (he planned to ship crofters to wild British Columbia; sheep farms in

Scotland being more lucrative than tenant farmers). You're going to Playland, driver says. That's gate 6 over there.

Café SVP | To lunch with A— at funky corner remnant of 1920s art deco, glazed terra-cotta stripes, pyramids and checkerboards — green awning a low-slung cloche hat. Inside, red vinyl booths and round stools on raised platforms. Rusty red walls. Off-beat food like rice and beans. Corn bread. Beet borscht. Peanut-butter and banana sandwiches. Salad of cheese and sunflower seeds. Through the hatch, kitchen help washes glasses under the tap.

A— shows night photos of derelict department store that's supposed to be made, for last 10 years, into low-cost housing. They've cut through eight floors a square chasm from sky to basement. The higher you go, the deeper the pigeon shit, the more the corpses. A— and friend wear bandanas over mouths and noses. Night bandits. Photographing stairs with oak banisters and flaking, tattered wallpaper. Orange stains on green walls. Saw-cuts through hollow bricks. A fluorescent light dangles from torn palimpsests of store decor. Dark tunnels zoom out from caked floors and stark columns like a set from a murder movie.

Then A— shows photos of a white bungalow, his childhood home, in sunny empty creek beds and hills of ponderosa pine. Stucco walls, trimmed shrubs, basketball hoop in the driveway.

Sir,

I am eyes. Photosynthesis in leaves. Spots for catching photons on planaria. Cups of pigment catching sunshine, moonshine, anything shine in limpets, flatworms, clams. Pinholes in a chambered Nautilus. Curved mirrors in scallops and wolf spiders, and peering out between shells of a seed shrimp. I am hundreds of lenses on trilobites and dragonflies. Cameras with shutters in deer, mice, raccoons. Light-guiding filaments deep in the sea. Or javelin spookfish, two eyes on the underside, two eyes on you.

I am all eyes. You are one eye. You are one word. I am words, speaking a million languages. The same code that gives eyes to the fruit-fly gives eyes to you. Words flowering in variant ecologies. And words are eyes for seeing. Words dream, but meaning loves its cardboard gods. Meaning mirrors point of view. Words are blind at their centres, words call out, they summon.

Rambling tapeta,
Geo, Vancouver

Vacuum Pan |

As water evaporates, crystals form. Sealed in bolted / riveted steel. Two hours to boil a 40-ton strike. 1975, workers off the job for 10 months, the second one ever.

Strike: (1) to remove from the record; (2) to form e.g. by stamping / printing coins; (3) to fall upon, the argument struck her fancy; (4) to discover — viz. she struck oil, then gold. 1976: sugar factory buys oil and gas company — $48 million, then a petrochemical company. Pays $44 million in dividends 1988.

Quashee: six days a week, daylight to dark, underfed. Plantations gave workers only hand tools to farm with. Childish tasks breaking resistance, numbing intelligence.

Saved by Sugar — three WWII soldiers stranded at sea in a zodiac on a poster; sugar has kept them alive. BUY A BOND — VICTORY IN JAPAN. *Successful Hostesses use BC Lump Sugar. This dainty and convenient cube.* Icing, berry, golden yellow, best brown, crystal diamond. *Makes foods more appealing, helps maintain a balanced diet ... the best in the world.*

"The most heinous Negro crime was rebellion or conspiracy against the white ruling order." *Sugar's peacetime performance promises to be little short of amazing.* "Every Negro caught during this rebellion was killed — burned alive, torn by dogs, or drawn and quartered." *The industry is confident that sugar will become as common to the manufacture of things as coal and petroleum.*

Granulator |

Sugar factory buys Fiji cane plantation, buys Alberta beet plant, buys Ozama plantation, buys Manitoba Sugar. Builds beet factories, mounting *campaigns* of lumpy roots to fill box-car after box-car bulldozed into cossetters and diffusion batteries to divide syrup from the beet-root "cossettes." Pampered pet lambs; every beety whim and fancy catered. Old English cottage-dwellers.

Dutch standards grade crystals as chocolate, coffee, brown, yellow, sand. For refinement into white. Laws, which said "brutish slaves deserve not ... to bee tryed by the legall tryall of twelve Men." Who slogged beside boiling evaporators, and turned the cane-crushers' huge steam-valves with tiny steering wheels. Who make "necessary" adjustments to lowest price. In current parlance, "restructuring revenue-sharing with beet growers." Meaning growers got less / and left to government subsidy.

Glucose, fructose, dextrose, turbinado, amazake, sorbitol, corn syrup. Remain competitive. Campaign: from Latin *campus;* to launch military action. Compare encampment, scamp, champion.

Spinning 1200 RPM, centrifugals drive the syrup from crystals. Sweetland cloth takes out impurities. Screening makes every crystal — Mexican, Brazilian, Peruvian, Trinidadian, Argentinian, Australian, Cuban, Fijian — precisely the same.

On behalf of myself and associates I beg to lay before you a proposition to establish a sugar refinery ... provided that the city ... shall vote a bonus to the company of $40,000.

Sir,

A tree cannot be industrious. A forest is not diligent. Nor is a pride of lions conscientious. Humans and ants invented industry and slaves. Clients and puppets. The killing of birds with stones. The having of irons in fires and fish to fry. For bigger and bigger piles of eggs. Yet the average ant is idle (a running engine of what gigantic engineering) most of the time — standing still, grooming, or walking around aimlessly (to humans); aimfully (to ants) of ease of being. Of breath. Of respiration. Of realness on foot under the sun, which human industry calls lazy wasteful slothdom. Slavemakers, then, war-liking parasites of captive playthings. Profit tautologies. Sleeveless errands and goose-chases.

Where is consciousness? Tiny stage for vast audience of unconscious watchers, colonizers, memory-carriers shaping the seen. Remember peppery, ginger ant-thoughts evolving slave states again and again. Warring aztecs destroying all other aztec colonies in the same cecropia tree. Sir, you could remember ribonucleic acid.

Red sky at morning,
Geo, Vancouver

Value Village | Old Super Value building laminated arches swoop up from ground and down again over an acre of floor-space. Once held aisles of bigger and better merits: viz. Kraft Dinner and Kellogg's sugar-coated breakfast. Now Canada's Favorite Thrift Store — banner across back wall. Racks of used shirts / pants / jackets / house-coats spread out north east south west. Shelves of dishes. Walls of cardboard landscapes. Framed. For the village of values where human heads drift in mazes of racks — small, medium, large — pink, blue, black. 1.99, 4.99 — everything.99. Humans with shopping carts flip flip flip thru hangers — long-sleeved, short-sleeved shirts. Baggy black jackets. One with tassels and epaulettes. Wide lapels, narrow lapels. Velvet. Pin-stripe. Zipped. Hooked. Please do not disturb cart stocker, sign barks near cordoned-off yard of Halloween. If I could take these down three inches — someone holds up trouser value. Does this hide my bum — a man with sports ethics. That's a jacket you'll never get tired of. On the back wall honourable stuffed animals and right-thinking jigsaw puzzles fill the shelves. Furniture! — a whole basement of worthy microwaves, computer monitors, toasters, mixers — thousands of decent and proper lamps. Near a wall of honest paperbacks, a boy practices his swing with a sensible baseball bat.

Evening | Night falls. Switching off legibility. Something evening things up. The giant ball turning, humans bolted to it like lint with static electricity. Sinking into darkness as the sun sinks in the sea. Joggers, rollerbladers whiz past. Evening sun tingeing faces, hands gold — tingeing the people in metal chairs sunk in the sand with words cut out of them. Chairs or people — words cut out — and what's left over evening things up?

English Bay beach, Squamish said Eeyulshun, good footing, before English — can you stand on words? Silhouette players volley silhouette balls over nets. The words, old changing-rooms, dig into a hillside where Joe Fortes pitched his tent, taught kids to swim off a raft floating in red-gold water. *C'mon now, kick — kick!* Arms and legs splash the surface.

Park artists range out pictures on little tripods. The cat lady with big smiley cats on pink backgrounds and blue and red roosters on yellow. Someone's painting cartoon rocks in dayglow orange — towers of boulders the rock-stacker makes out at Steetewuk. Someone's painting jigsaw landscapes — words, too, floating rafts — yellow, blue, green — how real is this painted scene a saxophonist riffs to a portable speaker.

A crowd of Russian old folk hangs around two benches, arguing heatedly. Then a bruiser / brooder in a hammock between stout alders. Hulking shoulders and elbows on hulking knees, his radio scratches in the grass. He gulps from a paper cup and stares at couples, families strolling along. Friends chatting about work. Two men holding hands, looking at the sunset. It costs $38.00 a month a woman says, pleased at her purchase. On life. Sun sinking, sinking, sunk. Something bobbing on wavelets' silver surface — a log, a deadhead — incoming tide. A human head — in the shimmering bay and bowl of smoky mountains. Swimming alone. As Oppen said, as far as she dares.

Shadows lengthen. A heron flies low, back to the heronry or the top of a condo tower. Head on long neck tucked back to body. Wide wings, long beak. Clouds' orange strands streak across greeny sky — long tracks locks of hair. Reach up. Touch the fibrous cotton's strange striations over giant river mouth.

Red sky at night sailor's delight. Red sky in morning sailors take warning.

Sir,

I am not city, not form, not named, not bounded. I am not purpose, not use. You are intentional. I am unintentional. You are the driver, I am the driven. You the actor, I the action. You the presence, I the absence. You the marker, I the mark and the marked, the murked, the mucked, the marched. You are the breather, I am the weather. You the ship, I the sea.

You build churches. I am not church, not stated, not victories. You think, you conceive. I am thought, conception. You search. I am intelligence. I am nonproclamation. I am unclamorous. You have things. I am without ideas. I am remnants. Un-archital.

You are grammar, graphage. I am unparsable departure. You paint landscape. I am uncivilized. You are a portrait. I am intractable. I am not big news. I am not patient or indicative. I am not a clock or a confession.

Unopened, unclosed,
Geo, Vancouver

Baptizing Mars | Are things more than their namey dreams? More than a fight with monster chaos where blood's the price of order? Humans calling Martian places in fanciful Latin Oxia Palus, Ophir Chasma, Labyrinthus Noctis, Valles Marineris — the Mariner's Valleys in a sea of language.

The positive or relative situations of all coasts, capes, promontories, islands, rocks, sands, beaches, bays, ports will hereafter be stated as true, or by the world, Vancouver wrote in his Journal of Discovery. He loaded sheep at Cape of Good Hope. For food. Seamen eating biscuit, sauerkraut and portable broth for weeks. Eighty men in a 100-foot boat. Slaughtering. Sleeping. Shitting. Making lunar observations.

A Voyage of Discovery — a passage through matter to something transcendental, above all, and absolute, R— says is IN language — not high as the sky. Gods like Mars not out there but in the word-dreams humans fancy. To make the real. To make the sanitized logic of money. Of divine right. Of sovereignty. The whole planet divided into nations, every one buying cheap, selling dear. Dreaming wealth of nations getting bigger and bigger forever.

He set out to map the true. He measured compass variation with 20 sets of azimuths. As though measurements would protect him from the dream. He found his chronometer eastward of truth. *Rain and haze obscure every object ... no indication of the vicinity of land.* Which Cook called No Body Knows What. He named it Some Body Knows What. He named it Escape Point, Doubtful Island, Port Desire, Possession Sound.

Yet true places are never found on any map, Ishmael says in *Moby Dick,* speaking of Queequeg's island Kokovoko far away to the West and South. Names' apparent islands make holes in the world.

Dragonfly **ı** *The ways will be more convenient if they are made everywhere equal; that is to say, that there be no place in them where armies may not easily march* (Palladio).

Cities must have streets and the streets must form grids. Beginning with Roman centuries (time cuboidal) 2400 feet squared, each century a hundred land holdings. Gridiron colonies — the military *castrum* — walls and gates to great *cardo* and *decumanus*. Crossed. All over Europe. All over the new world north-south, east-west strip-malls, freeways, shopping plazas, McDiners, McWarehouses.

Traffic so bad in Rome Caesar banned wheeled vehicles in daytime; noise at night drove Juvenal mad. 1563: the French parliament begged the king not to allow carts in Paris.

Before grids, there were folds, caves, crags, snakes of rivers, crooks of trees, rounds of yurts, corrals of sheep, fingers of land in the sea. Then rectangles — lots and lots of lots to sell. So much better if they are mid-air, no hassle of gullies, springs, swamps, sand or cliffs. *Orthogonic:* right-angled building. *Orthographic:* right spelling. For interchangeable cuts of capital-speak.

Something dark whizzes past the thought-pond. Bird. Whatever. Past a murk where tiny stemlets of algae cling. Fishy thoughts dart here and there to leaves, bacteria, worms, detritus falling in watery sun-shafts. Something dark hovers. Bird-egg body, long tail flashing blue / green electric stripes. Wing-blur over water, zips to leafy canopy, touches down to rusty iron birds on their rusty bath. Why must it look like a helicopter or a helicopter like it?

At night in nowhere / anywhere city. Think of Juvenal's insomnia. Think of Vancouver walking. Sailing. Navigating. Where. To find coral growing high on cliffs far above the sea. Four feet tall thick crusty branches. Maybe cities are coral. Human coral. Made of thousands of meaningless parts. But too much closure here in metaphor. As though language makes a movie and strolling through the words you watch pictures. Whereas words act in plays among themselves. And the mind's a dragonfly.

Sir,

You are the prime meridian. Imposing your measures everywhere on every living being. Your latitude and longitude dream of reference points. Forty-nine degrees, seventeen minutes by a hundred twenty-three and six. A few seconds southwest. Each second worth so many feet in space-time. Each foot a pinprick in reason's ownership, barred from all other feet. All other measures that walk, crawl, slither, swim, fly, wade, gallop, ooze. The capacity of anything to take action, take steps, make laws drumming for good measure. Make diameters, parameters, perimeters symmetries menses, monthly moons.

You squirp, you burble. You click your adding machines. Repeat your honey-dances. Squirt your pheromones. You dream, you imagine you mean, you signify. Repeating your dances and clickings, you dream that you choose. Copying, recopying, mimicking, aping. How to eat with a fork, how to wear clothes, how to get money, how to get girls.

Sir, I write without significance. I am the writing. I am writing you.

In the dark,
Geo, Vancouver

Living Waters ı

One second = 101 feet going south from Vancouver Harbour. Hastings stretches east, west, six seconds south of 49° 17 minutes — commemorating British rear admiral whose ship was *Zealous.* Twelve seconds (66-foot kind) west of 123° 5 minutes stands the Buckshon Pharmacy where addicts pick up their methadone. Then, heading west, comes the Woodbine Hotel Housekeeping and Sleeping Rooms. At 786 a steel mesh door. 784 a steel gate painted blue, locked before an empty storefront. On the walls a painted desert with rippled sand and painted palm trees. *Closed. Please come back in 10 minutes. No smoking* — City Health By-law. Here, 10 minutes can be several years.

782, purple paint, Living Waters Jesus is Lord Pastor Gloria. Blue and white, *Jesus is Lord over Skid Row.* Prayer Canada, red and white. Monday, Revival; Tuesday, Pastor Gloria preaches; Wednesday, Revival; Thursday, Pastor's day off; Friday, Shopping; Saturday, Service (food); Sunday, Service (food).

Rows of chairs with turquoise seats look to piano and microphone, a wall with two painted gulls and Niagara Falls cascading through clumps of cedar and fir. Rotary fans in the hot September day turn their fan-heads this way and that. A ficus plant with basketball and green starfish scrunches its leaves against the storefront glass. But the starfish is the leaves on a palm-tree balloon.

Ball-cap, tattered jeans and т-shirt drifts out of Woodbine Hotel, says he works in Living Waters. *We give them donuts and coffee,* he says, *hot dogs in the summer, spaghetti and macaroni in the winter.*

Ministry of Human Resources ı

702 Hastings Street — one side a sweat-shop door. Behind iron palings, an empty baby-stroller and seamstress of oriental lineage at her machine, working through piles

of cut fabric. Lucky Golden Convenience, says other side of 702.

At Heatley Avenue, the Heatley block — Edward Davis H, once owned part of Hastings mill, another form of sweat. Squamish and Musqueam got $20 a month for 12-hour days. The mark of the beast.

666 Hastings: Ministry of Human Resources Employment and Assistance Centre. *Time Limits* brochure taped over the word *human*. A sleeping-bag lies on the wheelchair ramp. A woman rummages a bin for pop cans. Keyed Stubs says a box beside clerks swivelling chairs other side of glass.

Through the front door, one bare room with benches, bulletin board and rack of brochures: "the people this ministry serves are truly a resource." Rocks and trees, too — resources for extract industry. "Families with children who exceed their time limits will have their rates reduced by $200 per month." Brochures show smiling white people, speaking on telephones, circling help-wanted ads, hugging their brief-case and their child.

A stout wall divides clerks from "resources." Four of five wickets closed. A woman asks for her cheque, her baby screaming in its stroller. *Courtesy*, says a sign, *It works for us. It works for you.* Another woman comes in with two toddlers. Human Resources Canada offers training in anger management and the power of attitude. Pie-chart Career Goals with wedges of Personal Style, Significant Others, Labour Market and Educational Background.

And he causeth all, both small and great, rich and poor, free and bond, to receive a mark in their right hand, or in their foreheads: And that no man might buy or sell, save he that had the mark.

Sir,

Raccoons stand under trees at night, twisting leaves in their hands. They watch you with masks. You fence them out. You are not raccoon. You are not ratoon cane but the big first cane that makes the best sugar. You have language, raccoons have none. Though they could say the same of you in their purrs and whistles, clicks and yelps. You reflect, have reason and logic; raccoons have none. You think. So reasonably, reflectively, you choose who has reason and who doesn't. Who deserves medicine and who deserves death. Who gets Humvees and who gets a dollar a day. Poisoned water. A kidney snatched. Prison without trial.

Becalmed in a sea of stupidity or perhaps it is a hurricane, I cling to this: small islands cannot support big predators.

Evolution never plans in advance — its starbursts of emptiness,
Geo, Vancouver

New Albion **|** *Considering ourselves now on the point of commencing an entirely new region, I cannot take leave of the coast already known* (George Vancouver). The ship rode all night by the wind, anchored in thick rainy weather. He was looking for white land, or chalk cliffs. He found Destruction Island and Lookout Point. *The country had the appearance of a continued forest as far north as the eye could reach.* He saw a sail to the west, the first vessel in eight months. He saw thousands of rocks, conical, flat-sided, flat-topped and every other shape of the imagination. A shallow bay, the feet of inland mountains, a point, an island-dot lying off it. Was it Cape Flattery? That flattered Cook's hopes for a harbour. Or was it a sandy beach. Of a bay Cook's Discovery and Resolution stood into. Cook seeking a pretended strait of Juan de Fuca, but saw *nothing like it, nor is there the least probability that iver any such thing ever exhisted.* On the long lost coast Drake named New Albion. Albino. Albumen — not white to the egg — only white to humans. Alba almost palindromic. Able was I ere I saw Elba. Not Alba. But in imagination's geography. A projecting point at Cape Disappointment — immediately within the point, the gist, the purpose, the country more elevated — the point answering to Mr. Meare's Cape Shoalwater but from the adjacent country rather appearing to be his Low Point. Our voyage irksome for want of wind, our curiosity much excited to explore the promised expansive mediterranean ocean. Though other explorers' large rivers and capacious inlets are reduced to brooks insufficient for our vessels. Except one at latitude 47° 45', the ancient relation of John De Fuca, the Greek pilot in 1592, where Spaniards found an entrance that in 27 days brought them to Hudson's Bay.

Demolition jaws bite siding and studs — a lo-rise on Venables Street, Captain Cavendish, of the 74th Highlanders. Floor boards snapped. Splintered ceilings wrenched from windows. Layers of torn-off ship-lap, stucco, vinyl. Demo — demon — de monstrate — democracy — demolish — molecules unmolar. Steel links caterpillar / crush wreckage. Breaking, jerking the old Captain in his tarnished braid, his radishes and whiskey. Downtown, the moguls prop grey stone slabs and cornices of old banks around their construction pits, buttressing with steel i-beams lords of thin-air-land.

Fallujah: hospital wall full of holes the size of bricks — one hole like an ox with its head down. Two men study the wreckage. US troops killed 8 US-trained Iraqi police. *The Fourth World War* papers say. In Baghdad, thousands mourn the Ayatollah. Coffin on the back of a flatbed truck draped in thick black cloth. Coffin almost empty. Merciful God, al-Hakim has gone. The bomb destroyed all except one hand with the Cleric's watch and wedding ring and the pen he frequently used.

Sir,

At sea, to see go polar. Be arctic or antarctic. I am neither and all. Gondwana breaking up in rifts, basins, currents — Gone Wonky spreading ridges, sucking trenches — continental drift-wood, so many kelp bladders afloat on radioactive starfragment. Sea-trash and tide-wrack, slowly swirling on molten soup, clump, drift south, then scatter, drift north. Clump / scatter, south / north / south — breathing. Dinosaurs rise, trample, suddenly choke, die. Rat-size mammals rise, trample. And humans go forth, rise, multiply.

At sea, I drift in my boat, my small rocking boat of history, my small boat of seeing. Antarctica sliced in pie wedges. Only the sea left, beyond human grasp. The sea and the sky. I collect leafy sea dragons. Bongo-beating angels. Chameleon-wizards kissing. Magic scales for fish-eyes. Give-away festivals. Fields of utopic underwear undoing. Symphonies of dreamers. Buffoons, clowns, leprechauns. I collect streets, cubbyholes, cries and chattering tongues. Banshee alleys gypsy memory nomadic questation.

Midden mind,
Geo, Vancouver

Homer Street

Going North on Homer Street, past old, bay-window Homer building and '70s diner. People cross rainshiny pavement under clouds, sun, the north mountains squeezed between skyscrapers. What would Odyssey poet sing here? For Homer Street's namesake Joshua Atwood Reynolds H, sawmill owner, 1858, High Sheriff of the New West, proclaiming humans on tiny faraway island owned mountains to 500 miles east, 1000 miles north.

Next door, a window-washer 30 storeys up sits on his little bench dangling from ropes. Reaches round behind him to bucket below seat, plunges in squeegie, pulls it back rickety rope-joggle, rubs it over the big glass between him and mill owners. Who plant trees on top of skyscrapers' glass trunks up to spreading lips, a torch flaming high in the sky *acer macrophyllum.* And Cheshire raccoons.

Borrowed Words

come on grapevines. Humans chirp / chatter, utter other, R— says. As Dante loves Beatrice, so humans language otherhood's otherland. Dusky golden light filling his writing room. Velvet carpet, red / violet. A globe, an oak desk, a typewriter. On a brass easel, an Indian tapestry where two skeletons dance. Reminding me, he says, of what's to come. Leather-bound books on the walls. Above book-shelves, pictures of Dante and companions in poetry. The desk covered with books, fringed lamps, gold ornaments, wooden boxes containing lockets and rings. Marble statues of angels. The windows shuttered, a sorcerer's cave of verbal architraves. Everything stock still except shape-shifting shadows. Chamber of dreams, passions, cravings, sorrows, delights of mind, voices of poets rattling chattering hailing the world — 2500 years of voices. Here meeting in velvet violet dream-ship. Fish reaching for the surface of what imagines humanity. Nosing water's silvery underside, never seeing the whole, what imagines all. Only glimpsing beyond fishy rhetoric possible music of the spheres.

Sir,

I loved you.

Rock became bacteria became plants became animals became monkeys, gibbons, chimps became ergasts became you. I became you. Loved you.

You lived willy nilly like ants, mice, microbes — a spreading dust / a pollen sailing everywhere, in caves, on plains, in forests. Raging with life. In the myriad living entities / my languages, you were another language / another utterance.

I uttered you. I loved you.

I sailed on in darkness,
Geo, Vancouver

A Note on Sources | In his *Arcades Project,* Walter Benjamin comments that "arcades, winter gardens, panoramas, factories, wax museums, casinos, [and] railroad stations" are examples of "dream houses of the collective." He means in this term the ways in which a society collectively imagines, without awareness or questioning, certain values and histories, which it represents in the things it produces. "Museums," he says "unquestionably belong to the dream houses of the collective. In considering them, one would want to emphasize the dialectic by which they come into contact, on the one hand, with scientific research and, on the other hand, with the 'dreamy tide of bad taste'." In his researches Benjamin sought to gain a "foothold ... from which to cast a productive glance, a form-and-distance-creating glance, on the nineteenth century." For the forms of our collective dreams, as Benjamin points out, "allow us to recognize the sea on which we navigate and the shore from which we push off."

Other sources include:

E Adnan, *There*

N Bowditch, *American Practical Navigator* (1962)

M de Cervantes, trans. B Raffel, *Don Quixote*

G Davenport, trans., *Herakleitos & Diogenes*

R Dawkins, *The Ancestor's Tale*

R S Dunn, *Sugar & Slaves*

H Ferriss, *The Metropolis of Tomorow*

T Flannery, *The Eternal Frontier*

L Hejinian, *The Language of Inquiry*

E Hoyt, *The Earth Dwellers*

D Hume, *A Treatise of Human Nature*

J Ingram, *The Burning House*

J Jacobs, *The Economy of Cities*

H Kalman, *Exploring Vancouver*

W T Keeton, *Biological Science,* 2nd ed.

S Kostof, *A History of Architecture*

L Margulis and D Sagan, *Microcosmos*

J S Matthews, *Conversations with Khahtsahlano*

J S Matthews, *Early Vancouver,* 2 vols.

H Melville, *Moby-Dick*

S W Mintz, *Sweetness and Power*

L Mumford, *The City in History*

F Nietzsche, trans. G Handwerk, *Human, All Too Human*

F Ponge, trans. M Guiton *et al., Selected Poems*

M I Rogers, *B.C. Sugar*

J Schreiner, *The Refiners*

T Snyders, *Namely Vancouver*

G Vancouver, *A Voyage of Discovery,* 4 vols.

W C Williams, *Paterson*

Acknowledgements

Acknowledgements ǀ I am very grateful to the editors of the following journals and magazines who have published parts of *Nightmarker: Windsor Review, Bongos of the Lord, How(2), Oban, Doppelganger, Stylus Poetry Journal, New Yipes Reader, The Golden Handcuffs Review, Event, Damn the Caesars, Tinfish, The Capilano Review, The Walrus* and *Canadian Literature.*

I would also especially like to thank the following people whose comments, suggestions and encouragement made this book possible: Jacqueline Turner, Fred Wah, Daphne Marlatt, Erin Mouré, Aaron Peck and Robin Blaser. At NeWest, Doug Barbour has been extraordinarily helpful in editing the initial manuscript, and Lou Morin and Tiffany Regaudie have been energetic supporters. I am very grateful for this, and I would like to also thank Robert Kroetsch and other NeWest readers for their invaluable support and suggestions. As always, to my first reader Peter Quartermain goes my deepest thanks, for he makes everything possible.

At age eleven, Meredith Quartermain left her home in Ontario and travelled across Canada with her family to the tiny, one-time silver boom community of Argenta, British Columbia. There she developed a strong sense of place that influenced her writing and remained with her during her studies at the University of British Columbia. In 1983, Quartermain was commissioned to write a history of York House School, which prompted her exploration of Vancouver archival materials and pioneer narratives.

Quartermain is the author of several poetry collections, including the 2006 BC Book Prize for Poetry winner, *Vancouver Walking*. She is also the co-founder of Nomados, a small literary press in Vancouver.

For the full poetic experience, listen to pieces from *Nightmarker,* read by Meredith Quartermain online at www.newestpress.com.

Or, check out Quartermain's *Vancouver Walking,* winner of the 2006 BC Book Prize for Poetry.

"Walking cinemas, civic memory tours, these poems are sites for the eruption of public history chronically denied but there as trace in the very names that mark our streets. Meredith Quartermain's observant eye tracks what underlies or surrounds our daily routine, she sees what routine blinds us to, and in the process constructs some wonderfully trenchant slices of contemporary city life."

I Daphne Marlatt

More prose-poetry from NeWest ⅰ

Paper Trail by Arleen Paré
Shortlisted for the 2008 BC Book Prize for Poetry

Frances, a manager for a large corporation, appears to be very successful. However, Frances suddenly finds her peace of mind unravelling as she becomes overwhelmed by the destructive bureaucratic nature of the work world in which she lives. Frances starts to lose small body parts, hears mysterious Lieder music booming throughout her workplace, and obsesses over the caymans that guard her office building. Meanwhile, her alter-ego has regular conversations with the ghost of Kafka, who is writing the manuscript in which Frances appears. Written in prose-poetry, *Paper Trail* questions the rat-race work ethic many of us adhere to, more often out of necessity than choice.